Avoiding My Merry Birthday

SONJA GUNTER

ISBN: 979-8-88653-073-5

Published by Satin Romance
An Imprint of Melange Books, LLC
White Bear Lake, MN 55110
www.satinromance.com

Published in the United States of America.

Cover Design by Caroline Andrus

CHAPTER
ONE

"Ten minutes, Miss White."

"Okay, thank you, Mr. Rouge." Gloria sighed, the end of another day for some, but not for her. She brushed a stray strand of her brown hair from her cheek and hooked it behind her ear.

The artificial pine Christmas tree next to the store's exit caught her attention. It flickered in the now dim lights, and beneath it were red and white wrapped packages. They almost appeared comical or ridiculous along with the never-ending holiday music blaring through speakers in the ceiling.

"Bah humbug. 'Tis the season," she muttered under her breath.

She had every reason to be cynical, being one of those unlucky people to have been born on Christmas Eve, December twenty-fourth. Friends never wanted to go out and celebrate her birthday.

How could she blame them? They were either traveling to spend time with their families for the holidays or didn't have time with the Christmas rush. And then there were the non-

1

existent presents. When she did receive one, nine out of ten times it was a combination birthday and Christmas gift, or for one day, and the other day forgotten. She'd learned to simply tell colleagues and friends her special day was the twenty-eighth instead of the real date.

But today was a harsh reminder that besides turning thirty-five, she was alone.

No husband. No boyfriend.

Long gone was her childhood dream of finding Prince Charming. That fantasy had crumbled into never-neverland when her dad had walked out on her and her mom. The years since it happened hadn't healed the hurt and probably never would.

Gently, she tapped a wayward hanger in order to get it back in line with the others. Tucking a price tag here and there, because none should show per management, she wandered through the rows of clothes absentmindedly straightening them.

This was her life for the past two years.

A salesperson. Not even a manager or a key-holder.

So much for the expensive business degree she had earned. She only had herself to blame. The fast-paced executive jobs and career chasing sleazebags had ruined her outlook on what being successful really meant. That too was in the past, but she was moving forward.

Her mom said time would help. Something she didn't think she had.

The store's music began to play, "Baby, please come home. I remember when you were here..."

Gloria cringed. Not now. Not that song. It had been their song, hers and Jacob's, and triggered memories of what a fool she'd been for five years. She had actually been blinded by love—no blinded by someone she believed loved her. She'd missed all the signs that her fiancé, the newly appointed CEO of Marley & Associate's Company, had been cheating on her with of all people, her own secretary.

"Can I turn off the music?" The song hit the chorus lines, setting her nerves on end.

"Yes." Mr. Rouge looked up for a second and then continued punching the keyboard. "Five more minutes."

Hurrying to the counter, she bent over and flipped the switch. Thankfully, the offensive song ended, and the store became quiet, except for the sounds of Mr. Rouge closing the registers. He didn't even flinch when she walked past him.

Maybe it was time again to find a different job; one that would insure no male interaction. Men were on her list to ignore. She never wanted one in her life again for as long as she lived.

Gloria shook her head negatively. Wasn't this job to have been her safe haven? When she left Boston, her six-figure position along with her ex-fiancé and despicable secretaries, she'd chosen a new career that wouldn't involve men, a women's clothing store. It hadn't turned out very well so far.

Refolding a blouse that a customer had so haphazardly folded, she smoothed it roughly and frowned. So much for all her well-intended plans. It had only taken two weeks into the onset of her new career, at the Crat-Chit store, for things to go sour. Holly, the manager quit, and Mr. Rouge had been hired.

"Miss White, have you finished straightening the store?"

"Yes, I have." She responded by snapping to attention, not wanting to incur his short temper. It seemed she could bring it on easily more often than not.

"Are we ready to leave?"

The sarcastic reply she had been ready to deliver got caught in her throat. She looked around, certain he would find something, anything wrong or inaptly folded. Offering him a nod, when she found him simply standing there staring at her as if she'd grown horns, she then returned to the counter and removed her purse from the cupboard. Swinging the strap over her shoulder, she turned to him. "I am ready now, Mr. Rouge."

Inwardly she smiled at the use of his name. He had a habit of introducing himself to customers by using his full name, Stan Christopher Rouge. But if you put his initials together with his last name they made, Mr. SCRouge.

He and the character, Ebenezer Scrooge, from The Christmas Carol, could have been twins; both cut corners and overworked their employees. You would think he owned the company, instead of just being an employee himself. Since his first day as manager, several employees had quit, and she'd been expected to take on the slack each time. Which she had done of course, with no extra pay or recognition and she swore at herself for allowing that to happen.

The sound of metal scraping, shifted her attention toward Mr. Rouge who held the front door open. Gloria walked outside, stopped, and waited for him to turn on the alarm and lock the doors.

"Remember we open at seven a.m." He buttoned his suit-coat and smoothed down an invisible wrinkle.

"Yes, I know."

They were probably the only store in the world that opened on Christmas Day. But it was a holiday tradition and more of a private five-hour event for the store's best customers. Only invited guests were able to shop and receive the gifts the Crat-Chit company handed out.

It was sort of fun with the high energy and festive atmosphere, she told herself. The plausible excuse wasn't convincing. The real reason she agreed to work was because the company gave out the annual bonus and two free articles of clothing to all the employees. She needed both right now. The bonus in her bank account and the new clothes in her wardrobe.

"Try to arrive on time, not late like today," Mr. Rouge added.

She raised her eyebrows. One minute. He had the nerve to criticize her for that one stupid minute she punched in late today. "I'll be here bright and early. Have a good evening."

He didn't even bother to acknowledge her reply or wish her a happy birthday. She knew he had to have known it was her day being the manager. He simply turned on his heels and walked to his car. Jamming her hands on her hips, she huffed at his so obvious disregard of her as if she was nonexistent.

Goodness, the man needed to get a life. Or an attitude adjustment.

Sighing, she strode through the empty parking lot to her car. Since all the store employees weren't allowed to have their phones on the sales floor, she pulled her phone from her purse to check her for text messages.

Only the date and time lit up on the scene. No notifications of messages or missed calls. Zilch.

How could that be?

She'd been at work for more than six hours. Today was her birthday.

Pitiful.

She was the one who should get a life.

A few steps before reaching her car, Gloria pressed her

key fob. The usual beep didn't sound. What the hell? She aimed the key fob at her car door and pressed it harder; once, twice and a third time.

"Who am I kidding? Like that would make it work," she mumbled after doing it.

Nothing happened. No beep, no flashing lights.

"Crap," she said out loud. "How much worse can my birthday get?"

Looking around for someone to help, she found no other cars in the parking lot. Even Mr. Rouge was gone, he'd taken off as fast as he could.

She tapped her contacts on her phone and pressed AAA.

"Thank you for calling Triple A," a woman's cheerful voice stated. "How can I help you?"

"Hi." Gloria leaned against the side of her car. "I think my battery is dead. My member number is D4A21G92."

"I'm sorry you're having trouble. Thank you for your member number. Is this Ms. White?"

"Yes, that's me."

"Great. Let me check to see what our estimate service time frame is." The line went quiet. "Okay Ms. White, it looks like I can have someone there in an hour or so."

"An hour?" Gloria glanced at the screen of the phone for the time. "By eight-thirty. If that is the earliest, I guess that will have to do. At least it's in the upper seventies here in Naples, Florida. I don't have to worry about snow."

The woman on the other end of the phone laughed. "I'm in the Minnesota call center and its minus one degree here. Will you be safe to wait that long alone?"

"Yes. I'm in the mall parking lot and it's lit very well. A security guard should be around soon."

"Excellent, then I'll place the service call. I have your location as, 11535 Fashion Drive, Estero, Florida. Is there anything else I can help you with, Ms. White?"

"No, thank you. Have a Merry Christmas."

Ending the call, she manually unlocked the car door and got into the driver's seat. She tried the ignition, just for the heck of it, but the engine did not even make a grinding noise. She hit the steering wheel with the palm of her hand, and cried out, "Ouch."

It hadn't been worth the effort. She massaged her hand. Deciding to make the most of her time, she checked Facebook to see if anyone had left her a birthday message there. When none came up, she clicked off her phone and sat in a lonely silence.

An unusual bright light reflected in her rear-view mirror. Squinting, she tried to make out who had joined her n the parking lot. Was that the tow truck? How could help have arrived so soon? A low hum of music seeped through the air. Frowning, she tilted her head for a better angle to hear where it was coming from.

"Dashing through the snow, in a one-horse open sleigh..."

Grimacing at the driver's choice of songs, Gloria slid out of the driver's seat to watch a red tow-truck with a wreath on the grill come closer. The Christmas music was now blaring so loud she was tempted to cover her ears. The driver must really like the age-old song, she thought.

The truck stopped in front of her car, and she bent over to retrieve her purse from the car.

"Ho, ho, ho. I heard you're having a problem."

The deep voice struck a chord to a long-ago memory from her childhood.

"Aren't you into the holiday spirit?" She straightened and turned. "Sorry you had to come out on Christmas Eve—"

7

Gloria flung her arms outward to gain some balance as she felt herself falling. "Ohhhh, nooooo..."

Unable to evade the expected outcome, she held out her hand as she hit the ground hard. Her body jerked and then fell backward, causing her head to hit the pavement. Pain like a mother migraine surged from the back of her head to her forehead. She felt strong arms wrap around her upper body, lifting her. Before the expected blackness took over, she was able to fixate on a familiar pair of blue eyes.

"Nick?"

CHAPTER
TWO

FIFTH-GRADE CHRISTMAS BREAK, TWENTY-
FOUR YEARS AGO

A bright light made Gloria spontaneously squeeze her closed eyes tightly. Throwing an arm across her forehead as an added shield, she groaned and tried to collect her thoughts.

It took a few moments before she remembered that today was her birthday. Only one person, her mother, had sent her a happy birthday wish text, which she received before she went into work.

Work.

That's right, she had closed the store with Mr. Rouge, and they had walked out together. He reminded her to be on time in the morning.

OMG, I'm late.

No, she couldn't be. She hadn't been home yet. Her mouth tightened as the data she was processing became a dull ache of uneasiness. It nestled deep within her as clarity refused to come. Unable to focus, waves of thoughts after thoughts intertwined and became more confusing.

Mental images of her folding clothes, blended into colors

streams. A red tow truck became bigger and bigger until it was towering above her, and a Christmas wreath fell from its front grill. It floated down over her.

No. No.

The warped visions sent threads of alarm through her.

Using a breathing technique from her long ago pilates classes, she inhaled and held it for two seconds, before she released it. Repeating the exercise until she could feel a calmness come over her and her jumbled brainwaves rightened themselves.

She could picture herself and Mr. Rouge, who had just reprimanded her on the importance of time and not checking in late. He then walked away to his car, and she went to hers, but it hadn't started. She called Triple A and waited for the tow truck.

Then the bright colors and images faded. Everything went blank and dark.

Her mind resisted any memory to come forward. The harder she tried to remember, a piece would emerge and then disappear. The images were beyond her reach, gloating her to fail.

Irritated, Gloria bit her lower lip. If she couldn't remember anything, she had to figure out where she was and determine if she had suffered any injuries. She ignored the thoughts that all this was some sort of a dream.

She wiggled her fingers on her arm that shielded the now nonexistent light from her eyes. Each finger moved without any pain or problems. Satisfied, she removed her arm from her forehead, but kept her eyes shut. And as she did, Christmas music filtered into her mind.

That's right.

Her thoughts were clearing again. The tow truck had

come, and the song, Jingle Bells, had been playing. She had been standing next to her car and reached inside for her purse.

She'd fallen. Her head had hit the pavement.

OMG. Nick, Nick Klaaws, her old school friend was the tow truck driver.

A long-ago emotion of delight emerged from the shadows of her heart. Disinterested in to figuring out why they were showing up now, she shoved them away.

If Nick had caught her, where had he brought her? To a hospital? How much time had passed?

Minutes?

Hours?

Days?

Clinging to the flickers of reality, little by little, Gloria opened her eyes. However, the fog that had covered her mind a few minutes ago was now encompassing her. There was no outline of her car or the tow truck. But she knew she wasn't in the mall parking lot or in a hospital room. She couldn't see anything around her even though her eyes were open.

A haziness now filled the area. If this was death or the afterlife it wasn't what she'd expected. Dismissing the notion she'd died, she frowned.

Where was Nick? He'd been at her side and had come to her aid.

Then she thought, of all the tow truck services, why his? They hadn't seen each other since her ex-fiancé had proposed. It was odd that their paths hadn't crossed in the two years she'd been home until today. All of a sudden, her mind burned with a rush of scenes of them together. Some were from long ago and some she couldn't remember ever happening.

Why was she thinking of him? It wasn't like they'd ever been boyfriend and girlfriend. They'd only kissed once and there had been a spark, but nothing had come of it.

Had it been fate that had sent him to her? Or was it just a coincidence that he was the tow truck driver sent to help her?

If that was the case, where was he, she required help.

"Nick? Hello, are you there?"

He didn't answer. Gloria squinted, thinking that would help see through the cloudy thickness. But it didn't work. No shapes emerged, or people.

"Help! Is there someone here?"

The sound of her cry pulsated through the fog into the emptiness. She waited and waited. Still, no one came or answered her.

I'm dead.

Considering the words, her mood changed abruptly to anger.

No, I can't.

She couldn't be. Her denial sounded weak in her mind. Even though she was a strong person, death usually had its own path.

"It couldn't have come for me yet," she repeated to herself.

Taking matters into her own hands, she took inventory of what she felt, sensed, and smelled.

No scents like the humid Florida air or diesel gas from Nick's truck filled her nose. Which led her to the assumption that she had to be inside in some sort of a room.

If she was in a room, where was this room?

Determined not to give in to her fear, Gloria placed her

hands flat beside her. She at once felt cold hard tile, not a soft bed, or the tar pavement of the parking lot.

With the second question answered, she shifted to figuring out if she could move. She gritted her teeth in determination and slowly sat up. The white fog that surrounded her turned to a mist and objects materialized.

A metal desk popped up out of nowhere to her left and she counted three walls that were painted white. She blinked feeling lightheaded as she peered around the room. Her mouth dropped open when a large black chalkboard just appeared and covered the fourth wall, behind the desk. Rubbing her eyes, she twisted around in order to see behind her.

She was without a doubt in a room, but one with no door. The meaning of a room with no doors diminished her excitement. She succumbed to the possibility; she'd died.

If she was in the afterlife, why was hers a classroom? She'd never been a teacher or taught any classes. Dead or not, she wasn't going to take her new life sitting on the floor.

Ready to begin a self-evaluation, she stood and wobbled. Gaining her balance, she wiggled her arms and then her legs. Nothing seemed broken or injured. Next, she reached behind her head and felt her scalp.

Unable to locate a bump, Gloria frowned.

Confused even more, she pivoted around in a circle. Pieces of other things emerged, filling the empty spaces. One, two, three and four rows of desks became visible in the middle of the room. Shelves towered straight up out of nowhere against the right wall. Even a small Christmas tree sat in the front corner on a table, absent of presents.

"Miss White, I'm over here."

Disorientated, her pulse rate inched higher, and she held

at bay the faint threads of hysteria. As she twisted around, she came face to face with the person whose voice was eerily similar to that of her boss'. Her eyes widened as all kinds of questions swirled in her head.

"Mr. Rouge?"

It was him but wasn't him. Instead of the usual three-piece suit he wore to work, he was dressed in a casual blue polo shirt and stone washed jeans. His hair was slicked back, and a pair of thick framed glasses sat high on the bridge of his nose. Nerd city to the bones. Surprisingly, it fit him better than his stuffy business attire.

Blinking several times didn't work and her mind was working overtime in an effort to awake from this bizarre dream. When her several attempts to wipe him from her sight didn't succeed and the new scene didn't change, her nerves tensed. He still stood a few feet from her, and the classroom was still just that, a classroom.

"Yes."

Finally, he spoke. It was so like him to say as few words as possible.

"What's going on? Where am I—where are we?" she stammered in bewilderment.

"Nowhere."

"You're scaring me, Mr. Rouge." She awkwardly cleared her throat, afraid to meet his eyes.

"Ms. White, the wheels of time have us."

"Time?"

"I'm your guide—your spirit guide. I'm here for you."

"Spirit—spirit guide. So, I'm dying or am about to and this is my final musings."

"Come now. No, you're smarter than this. What do you see, Ms. White?"

On his probing, she glanced over his shoulders. Something flickered and a young girl revealed herself. She was sitting at one of the desks sobbing, with her arms folded and her head nestled in them. Then a boy appeared standing next to the girl. He patted her back. By the concerned look on his face, it was clearly a sign of comfort. And he wasn't the cause of the girl's distress.

"Okay, I give up. This is some sort of prank. How have you managed all this?" She threw out her arms wide. "I'm not sure. But make it stop."

Gloria reached into her pocket for her phone, but it wasn't there. Her only lifeline of protection was missing. Had she dropped it when she'd fell?

"Don't you recognize the classroom? Or the children?"

His probing gaze and emotionless voice chilled her. It was so different then her boss', Mr. Rouge's curt tone. She pursed her lips and stole a look at the kids. "Why would they be familiar? I was just in the mall's parking lot and a tow truck had arrived. Tell me the truth, have I died?"

Mr. Rouge rested his hands on his hips. "Why would you think that?"

Gloria pointed a finger at him. "You can't be real. The Mr. Rouge I know would never wear jeans. This whole scene is bogus. This is some sort of trick, and my imagination is running wild. Or this is the bona fide afterlife and I'm dead."

"Goodness, aren't you the cynical one. By the way, I'll touch on that problem later. For the record, I know you consider me a scrooge, but we are here for you. Think. Take a good look. This is a scene from your past."

"Okay," she shouted. "Now I know I've died. My past? You know nothing of my past."

He laughed. "Ms. White, you are very much alive. It

hasn't gone unnoticed how lonely you are. I'm your spirit guide to help you find your future. We'll commence with your past and then move on to your future. There is no need to show you how miserable your life is."

"I wanna wake up now," she shouted as fear gnawed at her self-confidence. "I've got to be dreaming. This isn't real." Reaching for her phone again, she remembered she didn't have it.

How she lived her life was her damn business. The tension that hung in the air had her second guessing who this man was, but she knew he undeniably was not her boss. She turned to find an exit, and rubbed her arms, as the temperature suddenly turned colder. The scene before her became active. The children moved and then spoke.

"Gloria, stop crying. He isn't worth it."

"Whattt do youuuu know. I told hhhimm I loooved him," she whimpered.

From the depth of her subconsciousness, she remembered saying those words. She halted her escape plan at the use of her first name. Very slowly, she turned to face the children who were suspended in time. An odd adrenaline rush surged through her. She blinked several times and the entire room transformed into her fifth-grade classroom.

The previous empty walls now displayed number charts, along with the alphabet in printed and cursive form. Several pieces of construction paper artwork were taped to the adjacent wall. There was no sign of her teacher, Mrs. Schmidt, or her other classmates.

"You can move closer." Mr. Rouge gestured with his hand.

Her head snapped to the right and saw him pointing at the children. "How did you make this happen?" She asked.

"This isn't possible? I have to be dreaming, no, this is a nightmare."

"I told you we're going on a journey through your past. This is stop one, as we go through a number of years. Remember who your friends are. Where is here, Miss White?"

"Maybe I'm in a coma and I'm hallucinating. I'll play along," Gloria said and regarded the scene quizzically. "This was—is my fifth-grade classroom. And that young girl is me."

"You're correct," he nodded. "So much heartache aimed at the wrong person. Watch and listen."

As she conceded, a glint of a memory surfaced. She didn't want it to, but for some unknown reason no matter how hard she resisted, it all came back to her in an explosion of feelings. This was a day she'd pushed into the never-ever think or reflect upon part of her mind.

Richard, a fellow classmate in fifth-grade, who'd sat to her right, was the boy she'd had a crush on. She would dream of him holding her hand and telling her how much he liked her. Even now the memory of Richard's smile fabricated butterflies in her stomach.

This particular day, she'd snuck out of the house, so her mother wouldn't see the makeup she had put on, or the expensive shirt she had begged her mom to buy. During class, Richard had intercepted a note she'd written to her girlfriend, Donnette, saying she loved him. He had laughed at her in front of the entire class and cracked mean jokes about her declaration.

Kids can be so mean. Being bullied has lasting effects on people. She was one of those people, a casualty of the time of when meanness wasn't considered malicious. It had been one of the turning points in her life when she ruled all men despicable.

After school that day, she'd stayed in the room, too embarrassed to face all of her classmates. Nick, who sat behind her, stayed with her.

"How can this be?" She turned away to look at Mr. Rouge.

"Ms. White, memories have a way of playing with one's emotions. It can warp what truly had occurred. Shall we continue?"

"Yes," she said adding. "However, my memories are very clear."

The kids unfroze, and Nick put his arm around her younger self. "Gloria, I'm sorry he doesn't feel the same way about you."

"Howww am I going to fffface him afterrrr Christmas bbbreakk? He's brrrroken mmmy heartttt." She stuttered through wrenching sobs.

"It's not that bad. No one will remember after Christmas break. I'll be your boyfriend."

The kids jerked and became quiet. It was as if they'd been put on pause. How was this happening?

"You and Nick would make a cute couple," Mr. Rouge said and smiled.

That smile sent chills down her spine. It was something she didn't see often on him. "Not sure what you watched. It wasn't him I had a crush on."

How young and naive I was once.

How wrong Nick had been. The humiliation lasted for months and even followed her into high school. "Is there more? If not, I want to wake up."

Once again, the scene before her came to life. Nick

continued to stay by her younger self's side, who was still crying.

"Boyfriend? You? I'm not in love with you."

Inching her way closer, she saw Nick's crestfallen expression. But as a young girl, sitting with her head cradled in her arms sobbing, she hadn't seen it then. How could she have been so cruel? She just did to him what Richard had done to her.

"Someday you will. When that time comes, I'll be there for you." The young Nick yanked a desk chair back next to hers and sat. "Tell me what I can do? Should I go fight him? I could put glue on the seat of his chair so his pants rip when he tries to stand?"

Her younger self raised her head and wiped her eyes. "No. You'll get in trouble. This is my problem. Thanks for staying after school with me."

Nick nodded. "Anything for a friend."

How was she to have known he had a crush on her back in the day, when he called himself a friend? Other memories of Nick always being by her side, helping her, and protecting her resurfaced. Why had they been so repressed?

"Miss White, I think we are done here." Mr. Rouge touched her arm.

She tried to pull free, but the lights flickered before the room darkened. "Wait! No, I want to stay. I want to see more. I need to see more."

CHAPTER
THREE
EIGHTH-GRADE -CHRISTMAS BREAK, TWENTY-ONE YEARS AGO

Her demand hung in the air.

Gloria continued to seize Mr. Rouge's arm. Dizziness caused her stomach to upheave before the pitch black lessened. In the distance, she caught the faint sounds of waves. Their rhythmic swish could lull a person into a void and that's where she felt she'd entered.

Then a ray of sunlight burst through the remaining darkness and a thick odor of saltwater assaulted her nose. "Where have you taken me?"

"This too should be familiar."

"How are you able—"

She swallowed hard. The earlier queasiness erupted in the pit of her stomach. She covered her mouth as a dry heave burst upward. Lifting her head, she looked for something to use as a centering point. But there was nothing, only gray fuzziness surrounded her. It was different than the one in the fifth-grade classroom.

Taking several gulps of air, she clutched her abdomen

with her free hand. "Do dead people feel sick? I'm not feeling so well."

"Sorry. I'll take it more slowly next time." Mr. Rouge tapped her shoulder.

Instantly, whatever had been ailing her vanished. Unable to believe it, she breathed inward normally. "This really has to be a dream."

"For the umpteenth time Ms. White, you aren't dreaming. You haven't died. And you're not near death. I've slowed time, so I can take you to certain events in your life. Now look, what do you see?"

None of what he said made sense. Maybe she had a concussion.

Slowing time?

Visiting her past? No one could do that.

I guess I'm pretty creative in my hallucinations.

Whatever type of fantasies she was experiencing she decided to play along. With one hand still clinging to Mr. Rouge, the scene before her revealed itself.

"I see the ocean. Sand. Sunshine." She pivoted to see what was behind her and gasped. "That's me."

Sitting under a sun umbrella was a slightly older version of herself than the one she saw before, wearing shorts, a tank top, and of all things, a Santa hat. The whole Christmas on the beach always seemed wrong to her but living in Florida that's what people did, palm trees with lights, bubble machines for a snowy effect, and plastic pink flamingos with Santa hats.

The scene in front of her wasn't triggering any memories. She'd gone to the beach many times at Christmas enjoying how the white sand gave an illusion of snow, minus the cold temperatures.

"Gloria, come see the shells. There are so many."

She angled toward the water to see who was talking to her younger self. Then she saw him, Nick. He too was a little older and stood just beyond the rolling waves. He'd grown taller and more muscular. His shoulders and arms were broader. On his head he wore reindeer antlers and was bare from the waist up. He had wrapped his shirt around his neck.

Why didn't I see in middle school how handsome he'd become?

When was this?

Wanting to piece together the scene before her, Gloria pressed hard to force some reasoning into her head. If the last scene had been fifth-grade, that would make this sixth or maybe seventh-grade. Her younger self didn't look older than twelve. She closed her eyes searching for a memory of this time and place, but the echoes of what had seemed stuck, remained unwilling to untangle.

Opening her eyes, the sounds of other kids laughing became clearer along with other things. More and more kids came into focus. They were all wearing Santa hats, reindeer antlers, or elf ears.

Oh my god.

She remembered. This was her eighth-grade field trip to the Naples Pier, their last day of school before Christmas break.

In the crashing waves, Richard the boy who'd crushed her heart years before, as if it had been a mosquito, was splashing water on the girls. Now as an adult, she didn't see why she'd ever lost sleep over his rejection. He'd turned into a smartass jock and someone she didn't have anything in common with or ever would.

Donnette was taking pictures with her phone. Her hobby

had taken a toll on their friendship. It had been a turning point, as she recalled. They'd stopped hanging out together and their late night girl to girl conversations had lessened too. This was the last year they'd been together since they had to attend different high schools.

What had become of her? Gloria composed a note to try and look Donnette up, whenever her imagination was done messing around with her mind.

"Don't be a beach bum, Gloria. Come out from the shade and enjoy the sun."

She focused on Nick as he approached the younger version of herself. He dropped a handful of shells into her lap.

"You know the sun isn't my friend. Besides, I've seen them before. Almost every day. This is a stupid field trip."

"Pick a hand," Nick said.

Without waiting for an answer, he plopped down next to her and held out his fisted hands to her.

"Stop being childish." She made a shooing gesture with her hand. "I don't want to play."

"Oh, come on Gloria. Just pick one."

If she had been paying attention to him, she would have seen the daring look he had given her. Instead, her younger self snubbed him by shifting away from him.

I certainly was no friend to him back then.

She continued to watch the two of them. Nick wouldn't give up, he moved closer with his fists outward still closed.

"Fine." She tapped his left hand.

Instead of opening the one she'd chosen, Nick opened both hands. One hand revealed a braided teal and yellow bracelet. "I made this for you. They're your favorite colors. It's a birthday present. Since we won't see each other until after it passes, I wanted to make sure you got it before your special day."

"A handmade gift. How nice."

The air stilled, and no sound came from the water or the other kids as Mr. Rouge squeezed her arm. The younger versions of herself and Nick were frozen in place.

Again, she'd been rude to him. Why?

Memories of him rushed forward. He had attended a different high school too, than the one she had. She didn't recall seeing much of him until her senior year. It was a day she didn't want to dwell on.

Mr. Rouge stated. "You had the whole world ahead of you, Ms. White. You just chose not to engage with anyone, to live in self-pity."

"No. This is the past. I left it behind. After my fifth-grade disgrace, Nick became a boy who was always nice to me at school. I didn't want his misdirected kindness to turn into anything."

"Misdirected?"

Mr. Rouge was right, why hadn't she seen his escalating attention? The question did intrigue her. Nick's adoration of her was now very obvious. "Okay, maybe not misdirected but for sure misguided. I didn't need someone to protect or love me."

"No wonder I was chosen, then appointed your spirit guide. Look at him. The boy who the stars had aligned for your choice was right in front of you all the time, and you ignored him. Do you see anything else?" He pushed her forward.

Losing her balance without his support, Gloria stumbled, landing face first in the sand. Spitting pieces of shells and bits of gravel from her mouth, she got to her feet and angrily swiped sand from her face. "That wasn't necessary."

Then she heard her earlier reply repeating itself softly over and over. "A homemade gift, how nice. A homemade gift, how nice. A homemade…"

After the tenth time, she couldn't take it anymore and covered her ears. It didn't help. The words still repeated themselves. Trapped in some sort of time loop like a broken record, she shouted. "Make it stop. Okay I get it. I wasn't nice. I didn't appreciate the gift."

Her nasty comment ceased, but the scene lingered unchanged. She and Nick were motionless. Gloria moved closer, saw the sadness, and hurt etched on his face because of her inconsiderate thank you. Even his blue eyes had lost their normal sparkle. It shouldn't have mattered but seeing it now, she regretted being so rude.

"Ms. White, the old saying about sticks and stones, can break your bones but words will never hurt you isn't true. Words can hurt. And they do."

Mr. Rouge was right again. Had she been a bully and never realized it? Nick had never complained to her. More rounds of now painful memories flooded her thoughts. He had always been there for her. Like helping her with math. Giving her lunch tickets when she didn't have one.

She had never thought of Nick as anything but a fellow classmate, just a friend. Now as an adult, Gloria could see he'd had feelings for her. She'd been so blind as a teenager.

What if she had paid more attention to him, been nicer? Would that have changed their lives, like Mr. Rouge had said about the stars choosing him for her?

No!

This was ridiculous. What she was seeing was the past

and that could never change. Mr. Rouge, her so-called spirit guide, didn't have that power. No one did.

"That's right, I can't change your past. These are the possibilities that you missed because you were mad at the opposite sex."

He shook his head in disappointment and his harsh words hit a chord deep inside her. Her fifth-grade humiliating refusal of a boy's love, had set her on a path of being unable to find love. Before the scene unfroze, he touched her shoulder. This time as they drifted through her past, people and places flashed before her.

CHAPTER
FOUR

T he flashes of her past were gone, only to be replaced with darkness and smells. A stench of greasy hot oil had Gloria wrinkling her nose. She hated that unforgettable odor with a passion.

Cringing at the reality of what this place represented from her past meant. It was her day from hell. She turned to face Mr. Rouge, who still had his hand on her arm, but couldn't make out his face. This was one birthday she'd hidden in the deepest part of her mind. Another steppingstone in her path of never finding love had been triggered here. Her fifth-grade rejection, by her first boy crush, had only been the tip of the iceberg.

Had Mr. Rouge read her mind with some psychic powers? Is that why he'd chosen this particular Christmas Eve to show her?

"I can't relive this moment." Continuing to brush sand off her clothes from the last scene with her free hand, Gloria added. "If I have to play along with this farce of a dream, pick a different birthday or Christmas, Mr. Rouge."

27

She waited for his reply. But none came.

Unable to see anything, her other senses were in overdrive. The awful greasy smell still besieged the air.

A ray of light filtered through the endless darkness, revealing where she guessed they were. Juicy Lucy's, the hamburger joint where she'd worked during her senior year of high school. The next thing that came into focus was the oversized menu sign on the wall. She didn't have to read it, because to this day she still knew it by heart. Why she did, she didn't know, but it was strange the things your mind chooses to keep.

As Gloria peered around the area, a person appeared behind the waist high counter. Unable to make out if it was a male or female, she tried to move closer.

"This wasn't on your resume," Mr. Rouge chortled and held her firm. "A fast-food employee."

"I was seventeen," Gloria tightened her mouth for a moment. "It was a way to earn money. Not all of us could go to college on a scholarship."

"No need to be sassy. I'm very curious to see what happens here."

And just like that the entire restaurant became as clear as the day she worked there. The motionless employee became the center of her attention.

It was her.

She flinched seeing yet another younger version of herself. Her long hair was in a ponytail and a stupid hamburger shaped paper hat was perched on her head. She was wearing a white shirt with a bright yellow apron over it. All part of her uniform. How she'd hated it then, and even now it looked ridiculous.

"I'm not—"

The sudden hum of machines and voices broke the silence, cutting her off. Her younger self moved from the kitchen window to the counter. A door chimed, announcing a customer had entered.

"Welcome to Juicy Lucy's," her younger self called out, not even turning to face the customer. "What can I get for you?"

"Gloria?" A deep male voice asked.

The way the person had pronounced her name with such a huskiness that was almost a caress, struck a chord of recognition, instantly. It could belong to only one person.

Nick.

Not wanting to watch, she lowered her eyes. "Please, Mr. Rouge."

The scene was put on pause. "What is it now? Your whining is very annoying, Ms. White."

Opening her mouth to reply, instead she took a deep breath and then released it. "Sorry, this place—holds too many unhappy memories. I want to leave."

"Many families break up, it's sad, I know. Google it sometime. The odds are not in favor of couples remaining together. You must stay and watch in order to move forward. You have to see and understand what you've missed."

"Families? How did you know this was when my dad walked out on my mom and me?" she asked curtly.

"I've been given access to your entire life. Your eighteenth birthday is a pivotal point. We can't leave yet. Our time here isn't finished."

Gloria's eyebrows rose. He did know things about her past. This was or had been her eighteenth birthday. She'd missed her father's phone call because she had been driving to work. It wasn't until she got to work and was able to listen to his voicemail that the day had turned to hell.

The message he'd left had been short, direct to the point and curt. He'd wished her a happy birthday, said goodbye, and promised to call when he got situated in an apartment. That day never happened. The hurt from his abandonment had turned into hate, not only at him but had spread into her opinion of all men. It had taken years for her to allow someone to get close to her again.

"No." She tried to free her arm and added. "I want to go home—back to my car."

His fingers tightened around her wrist. "You've been given a great opportunity to see your life from an onlooker's point of view. Take in everything, Ms. White."

After a few moments she studied her surroundings. Her earlier instinct had been correct. The person who'd said her name was Nick. Seeing her younger self's surprised expression, she wondered why. Could it have been because they hadn't seen each other since their eighth-grade graduation?

No. Her facial expression showed the corners of her lips almost curved into a smile. She didn't look angry. Her face seemed softened.

This is odd.

"Ms. White, are you ready to observe more?"

"Fine, I'll watch. Not sure why, the outcome won't change. My dad still abandons us."

"You're correct. But this is a learning experience," Mr. Rouge replied.

Together they moved closer to the counter. From her new position, Gloria noted how rigid her younger self's body was and the softened expression was gone from her face. She swallowed hard and lifted her chin. If this was her past, why didn't or couldn't she remember feeling all the mixed emotions she was seeing?

None of this could be real. It had to be her imagination playing tricks on her memories. Question after question formed in her mind. She turned to fire them at the ghost Mr. Rouge when the scene in front of them unfroze.

"It is, that's the name on my badge. Did you want to place an order?"

"Gloria White, from Three Oaks High School. I knew it. I'd recognize those beautiful sometimes blue and sometimes green eyes anywhere. What are you doing working on Christmas Eve, your birthday?"

Nick's flirtatious words had been ignored by her eighteen years ago. She remembered being angry at him simply for being a male. His acknowledgment of her birthday went unnoticed by her too. At this moment, hearing the conversation as an outsider like Mr. Rouge had pointed out, she wondered why he would've said her eyes were beautiful and how did he know they changed colors?

Then a major arc of understanding came to her. In the previous two stops, Nick had also remembered her birthday. He'd seen her as more than just a girl he knew. What had their relationship been?

"The big question, Nick, is what type of burger do you want?"

Something else seemed weird as she watched. Her younger self had responded by using his name. If they hadn't seen each other in four years, how had she known it was him?

Being forced to relive this moment, Gloria really got to study Nick. He had matured into a handsome young adult. As she observed him, she saw her younger self look away, another odd reaction she would have to analyze later. She couldn't help but appreciate how much he had changed since the last scene. His short black hair had a windblown look to it and his blue eyes held a glint of light in them.

She frowned and fought through cobwebs of memories.

"Gloria, is that how you greet the love of your life?" Nick said huskily and swiped hair from his eyes. "I haven't seen you in years and that's all you have to say to me?"

"Do you want to place an order? If not, move aside. I have things to do. Next." She motioned to the customer behind him.

He glanced over his shoulder. "Oh right, sorry. Give me a double patty Juicy Lucy with fries and your phone number."

"One burger with fries. And my phone number isn't part of the menu."

Mr. Rouge waved his hand, and everything halted.

She didn't remember Nick coming in or asking for her number. The only things she could recall in regard to that day was how angry and hurt she'd been, and her dad's voicemail.

"Why didn't you give him your phone number, Ms. White?"

Looking at her younger self's stern facial expression caught at her heart. "It wouldn't have mattered. I left for college the next month. I'd graduated from high school early. I didn't want any boy—man in my life. I saw first-hand how cruel they could become once they married you."

"Come now, Ms. White. Your father never treated you badly when you were growing up. He chose to exclude you from his life once you became a young adult. That's different. I'm sorry he did that to you. Did you ask your mother why?"

"No, I didn't," she snapped and lifted her chin higher. "Leave her out of this. She has always loved me. My dad..."

The scene reverted to a live stream, halting her rant. Several of the customers turned their heads, clearly in an effort to hide their grins over Nick asking for her phone number.

"I know, that's why I'm asking you. I'd like to ask you out on a date."

"Nick, I'd never date you even if you were the last man on earth. Your total is seven dollars and twenty-one cents."

Hearing her hurtful words weighed heavy on her. She cringed at her long-ago actions. Once again, she was a bully. The other customers shook their heads, clearly siding with Nick. As she watched him, he smiled, unaffected by her rude response.

"Playing hard to get. I understand." He slid a twenty-dollar bill toward her. "Keep the change. Buy yourself dinner on me as a birthday gift."

Before her younger self could reply he stepped away and the next guest took his place at the counter. Shoving Nick's change into her pocket, she took the next customer's order, but kept glancing in his direction. He ignored her stony looks and winked when their eyes met. Then a co-worker handed him his order. He gave her a one finger salute and walked out.

"Gloria, what are you thinking? Why didn't you give that cute guy your number? I left mine on his receipt," her co-worker stated. "If you don't want to go out with that good-looking hunk, I do."

Mr. Rouge yanked her arm. "It's apparent all the signs that have been given to you have gone unheeded. Or you refused to act on them."

The area around them darkened. She wiped at a tear as her gaze lost sight of the scene. "I didn't know. I never guessed he liked me so much."

"Ignorance isn't an excuse. Before we leave this time for good, I want to give you one last look at the man you so rudely turned away."

The inside of the restaurant disappeared, and they were outside. She spotted Nick standing by a truck. He kicked the tire, still holding his bag of food grumbling to himself.

"Someday, Gloria, you're bound to see me as the man who loves you. And has since grade school."

"Oh, my God," she gasped, covering her mouth with her free hand. His body and facial expression told her he had changed his mind and was primed to go back inside the restaurant. But he didn't. He did a one-eighty and opened the driver side door and climbed in.

How had she missed the fact Nick loved her? Her actions were unforgivable. She'd spit on him publicly, and without any regret.

I was so blind.

She reached out a hand to him. "I'm sorry Nick."

CHAPTER
FIVE
THIRTEEN YEARS AGO - CHRISTMAS EVE

L ike the three times before, Gloria felt like she was in a void. Not even sure that was what you called it, having never experienced such a thing before. The freakiness of the whole situation was disturbing. She prided herself for being open-minded, but this was stretching her resolve.

There were no sounds.

No images, only nothingness.

How Mr. Rouge was able to move her from scene to scene in her past she didn't know. The harder Gloria tried to make sense of it all, the more she became convinced this was all a hallucination.

But why play out the Christmas Carol story?

It had never been a favorite of hers, even though it did have a meaningful ending. The only solution she was able to come up with was, she had been thinking about the story before she and Mr. Rouge had closed the store.

The whole concept of being visited by ghosts had always struck her that Mr. Scrooge's mind had been playing tricks on him. There were similarities, but she chose not to reflect on the irrationalness of old works of fiction. Gloria fixated on the new area around her, determined to define something in the blackness.

"What wonderful part of my so exciting past have you brought to me now?" She stretched out her arms. "Where are you? I sense you but can't touch you."

A cold rush of air encased her.

"Ms. White, time is running short. We have many things to unlock yet."

His cold hand took hers and then as if a light switch had been turned on, her new surroundings metamorphized. They stood in the middle of a tar road. Stars danced in the night sky and the brightness of a full moon was the only source of light. She shuddered as a cool gentle breeze sent the palm branches cracking.

Gloria gripped Mr. Rouge's hand tightly, a little frightened now and she turned around for a better understanding of her situation. The deserted two-way highway stretched on and on from both ways. No vehicles in sight. The symbolism of a road leading to nowhere wasn't good. She had seen too many horror movies not to know when something bad was not far off from occurring. Drawing all the courage she could from every pore of her body, she was determined not to let fear get the better of her.

"I don't remember this from my past. I think you got something wrong," she gave a little anxious cough. "Since this is my dream, I want it to conclude."

As if on cue in some movie script, flashing brake lights blinked like a beacon in the dark ahead of them.

He laughed. "Should we walk closer?"

"No, that's okay. Shouldn't a new ghost be visiting me

soon? I'm sure it's past one o'clock, when will this nightmare end?"

"I'm your solitary spirit guide tonight. Come now, time is wasting away, Ms. White. You need to see who is inside the car."

Not giving her a chance to reply, he lured her forward as a car came into focus. Gloria detected how lopsided the car sat along the side of the road. Which could mean it had a flat tire.

Poor soul or souls. No one would be helping them soon on this isolated highway.

The night sounds lessened and was replaced by music playing so loud the disabled car shook to the beat. Soon the words of the song playing had her wanting to retreat. The words became even louder.

"I saw mommy kissing Santa Claus..."

Damn it. It is still Christmas.

Living in Florida with sunshine and green trees, all the seasons were the same. Gloria and Mr. Rouge continued to move closer to the car. The parking lights highlighted a sticker on the rear bumper. She stopped in her tracks when she read it.

Merry Birthday.

What the hell? Her heart raced. That was her car.

The one her mom had given to her as a birthday present. The bumper sticker had been kind of a joke between the two of them. Instead of Merry Christmas or Happy Birthday, her mom had combined the four words into two, Merry Birthday.

Was she to relive her birthday, a never ending a ray of possibilities, like the movie Groundhogs Day? But why?

Think!

When was this?

Then it registered, and bits and pieces were plucked from deep in her memory. This was the Christmas Eve she'd driven home from Boston to Florida. Her last exam the day before had ended late, so she'd left Massachusetts, in the early morning. After reaching central Florida, instead of taking I4 to I75 all the way to Naples, she'd taken the rural roads hoping to cut off time on the last leg. And had gotten a flat tire.

She struggled with the sense of right and wrong and glanced around. "I know how this night ends too. I've regretted my weakness ever since. Its relevance didn't exist until now. There, are you happy?"

"Ms. White, I have no feelings, but I'm sure what you're experiencing isn't regret. We have to let the scene play out. Look. Here he comes."

Gloria saw the headlights fast approaching on them—no, on the car—no, her car. "I'm begging you, can we leave?"

"But why? Don't you want to relive yours and Nick's first kiss?"

Mr. Rouge's self-satisfying mockery filled her with humiliation. She'd really never forgotten this night, no matter how hard she'd tried. And her lie a few seconds ago echoed in her head. Her body stiffened, knowing the imminent kiss was coming. A tingling in the pit of her stomach sparked quivers. Her whole body waited for something pending to happen.

Nick's words of love from the scene before fit into place. Gloria contemplated why he'd chosen this night to kiss her and how she had responded to that kiss.

The tow truck passed them and did a U-turn. Mr. Rouge tugged her to the driver's side door, just as Nick walked over to the car. Taking in how good he looked in his signature jeans and blue collared shirt with his name printed on the front, she gave her younger self credit for allowing the kiss to occur.

Why would she have viewed his jeans as a signature piece of clothing? Maybe because he was always wearing them when she saw him. No, it didn't make sense to her. She had only seen him like once every few years after grade school. They weren't close friends.

After their encounter at the Juicy Lucy restaurant, she had left a couple of weeks later. Boston University had been waiting for her. As she told Mr. Rouge, a boyfriend hadn't fit into her objectives. But this night, her twenty-second birthday she had abandoned her steel plated guard for a single instant. The anger aimed at her father had been a chain wound tightly around her and she'd loosened it.

"Ma'am, can I help you?"

The car window lowered, and the music level was reduced.

Her younger self had her hair pulled back, and she wasn't wearing makeup. That had been her normal look eons ago. She hadn't cared. With her class load there hadn't been time to impress anyone. Not that she would've, studying had ended any free time she had saved for herself.

"Thanks for coming—Nick?"

"Gloria? Gloria White? What are you doing on Hwy 17?"

Her younger self exited the car. "It's winter break. Driving home. Thought I'd save time coming this way."

She heard the tension in her younger self's voice. Why? Discarding some of those critical worries, she concentrated on Nick.

He held the door, the only thing separating them. "It's a

good thing I decided to take calls tonight. Didn't you learn how to change a flat tire?"

None of this could be real. Or could it?

The scene before was so clear, she could see the wrinkles in Nick's shirt.

Then time was thrust into overdrive and her younger self and Nick moved in accelerated motions. He stood, squatted, and repeated the actions as he changed the tire. She chatted and positioned herself in flirtatious poses. The stars changed positions like a time elapse movie. Even the Christmas music continued playing in high-speed.

Almost dizzy from watching the fast-paced movements, Gloria was thankful when the scene slowed and came to a stop. She closed her eyes, disinterested in seeing her imminent actions.

"Ms. White, open your eyes. The scene can't playout unless you are watching."

"Is that how this works? If I keep my eyes shut this whole thing will cease?"

"No, it'll wait until you open them. But like I said, time is running short. If you don't change your outlook on life, you'll become old and alone. Now open your eyes, he's waiting for you."

"What are you yakking about? Time? Old and alone?" She opened her eyes and stared at Mr. Rouge. "Who is waiting? I—"

The scene commenced at normal speed. Nick stood just a few feet from her younger self. "Happy birthday, Gloria."

"How—why on earth have you remembered it all these years?"

Nick wiped his hands on a towel tucked into his pocket

and took a step closer. "Because I told myself in the fifth-grade, I'd marry you someday. You are my soulmate."

"Stop it, Nick. We barely know each other."

"That's not true. We've known each other almost our entire life. Before you went to college you put me off, so I've been waiting for you to return home. Every so often your mom stops by the garage."

"You and my mom talk?"

"Yeah, when she drops off her car for an oil change," Nick chuckled. "You do come up in our conversations."

"She's never said anything." Her younger self folded her arms across her chest. "Marry me? That's an odd way to propose to a girl. You're so sweet. I'm not sure I'm the girl for you."

He took one more step, leaving barely enough room for her younger self to move her arms. "If you take that as a proposal, I'd be the happiest man alive."

"Whoa, take a deep breath, Nick. I didn't mean—hey, I'm not marrying anyone. I have to finish college. Maybe we can get together over the holiday. Chat. Go over the good old times. Thanks again for saving me."

The scene stopped, but she hadn't closed her eyes. How was that possible? Could Mr. Rouge control the events and lied to her?

"Ms. White why didn't you follow through with a get-together with Nick? You had to have known or sensed how he felt. Even I can see it and I'm a neutral bystander. It's very clear he's been attracted to you for a very long time."

"I didn't have time to socialize. I had to return to college. I couldn't initiate a relationship." Even to her ears the denial sounded disingenuous and pathetic. "Okay, I didn't want to."

The scene forged to life.

"You're welcome," Nick said and again wiped his hands. "Can I give you a birthday present?"

"A present? You have one for me, just in case you saw me? Really?"

He laughed heartily and took her hands, unfolding them from in front of her. "Yes, a gift. No, I didn't know I'd see you. It was, however, my Christmas wish."

Before her younger self could reply, Nick leaned in and kissed her on her cheek. He straightened, released her hands, and their eyes met for a moment. She wrapped her arms around his neck and kissed him on the lips.

"No more, Mr. Rouge. I know I shouldn't have led him on."

"Led him on? You did more than that. You most certainly broke his heart."

Even now as Gloria watched her younger self and Nick kiss, she swore she could feel his lips touching hers. His mouth moved over hers softly yet demanding, reaching a part of her she hadn't known existed until now.

How could this be happening?

The great beyond or dream world shouldn't be able to make her feel things. Was this another part of her very active imagination?

What would have happened if she had hung out with him while she'd been home on winter break? Could a long-distance relationship have been able to survive? His confidence in pursuing her as his soulmate had unknowingly softened her anger aimed at men at this moment.

Would he have been able to have saved her from her own forthcoming heartbreak?

CHAPTER
SIX
NINE YEARS AGO - CHRISTMAS EVE

"Stop this." Gloria pinched herself as the nothingness enfolded around her.

Gone were the images of her and Nick kissing. Having been caught off guard by the impact their embrace had on her, she felt drained. Lifting a hand to her mouth to feel her lips because they seemed swollen and were.

How could that be?

Nick hadn't kissed her. Well, he had, but it had been her younger self.

Mr. Rouge had been right. The kiss shouldn't have happened in the first place. She had never planned to follow through with seeing him during the holiday like they had discussed. Regrets assailed her for not saying goodbye to him before returning to college.

It had been the kiss that had led to nowhere. What a cold bitch she'd been.

"Ms. White, I wouldn't use that word, but I believe you are still one. You need to find yourself before we can exit this abyss of your never-ending sequences of life. The windows of hidden truths are running short on time. Nine years to be exact."

"Find myself? I'm right here." She pinched her arm again and grimmest at the pain. "See this is the real me. I want you to end this right now, Mr. Rouge or whoever you are. I'm done with playing out the Christmas Carol story."

He tapped her shoulder, and a delightful smell of freshly baked cookies engulfed the air around them. Her stomach grumbled, reminding her she'd only had a small bag of chips for lunch.

Peering into the new scene, she tried to center in on some of the objects. The things weren't able to give her a better understanding of where and when she was. "I'll need glasses before this night is through. Why all this secrecy? Is it for effect? If it is, you don't have to use it. Just make the scene appear if we are low on time."

Then like magic the area became submerged in light, almost blinding her. It took a few seconds before she was able to make out objects. A stove and sink indicated a kitchen. Then a table that was set for four and a woman taking something from an oven came into focus.

Gloria inhaled sharply, when the woman turned to place what looked like a cooked ham on the counter. "That's my mom," she shouted, halting the action. "This is my house. The one I grew up in. I told you not to bring my mother into this madness."

"Ms. White, she is fine. We are here for you."

"I don't understand any of this," she murmured. "The past is the past. It can't be changed."

"You are not embracing what I'm showing you. Your future depends on it. Now watch."

What was she supposed to embrace? The fact that she had

been a horrible person? Or that she was a shallow person? Reflecting on those questions gave her pause, and before she could say anything the scene resumed.

The kitchen, Gloria noted was decked out in Christmas decorations. Her mom was wearing her favorite apron with little gingerbread boys and girls on it. No one could say she lacked in having the holiday spirit. A Santa shaped cookie jar sat on the counter, along with a ballerina nutcracker and a bowl of nuts. Holiday music played from the television showing a fireplace and a sleeping puppy.

Good lord, my never-ending birthday. But which one?

"Gloria. Come help set the table."

A younger but older version of herself walked into the kitchen wearing a red short-sleeve dress. Gloria had to admit, she looked gorgeous. Not only in the dress, but with her hair gathered away from her face with strands hanging finished the look. A nagging memory of this particular Christmas sent a chill through her.

"Sorry, Jacob and I were wrapping a few last-minute gifts."

Then, in walked her two-timing ex-boyfriend—no ex-fiancé. She began to breathe hard, as the reason she had been so dressed up came back to her. This was the Christmas she had brought Jacob home to meet her mom in person, not via facetime. Realizing how romantically dazed she'd been made her sick to her stomach. Even after her long ago promise to never fall in love, she'd allowed Jacob to deceive her into thinking men weren't immoral.

Seeing him now, all his many flaws were as plain as day to her, right down to his unwavering lying eyes. As he emerged into the kitchen, he'd pocketed his phone. An action she'd missed years ago, but now became an important piece to the puzzle of his infidelity.

"Smells wonderful, Mrs. White. Will you permit me the honor of carving the ham?"

"Oh, no, that is my job," her mom stated.

The tartness of the reply, was an additional clue she'd missed years ago. Could her mother have seen through Jacob's fakeness from their first introduction?

As she tried to recall details, a conversation she and her mother had a few days earlier came full circle. Her mother had warned her sometimes love could be miss-guided. And that true love sometimes was right in front of you and not where one would expect.

Her mother's advice had sounded odd at the time, and she had simply ignored the guidance.

"No questions, Ms. White?" Mr. Rouge asked as the scene froze.

"This night is vague," she said and covered her face with her hands. "Okay, I'll give you this one. I'd like to see this one through. I've already caught a couple of things that now fit into place but hadn't at the time."

She lowered her hands and clung to his arm, not wanting the scene to vanish. This was the day Jacob had proposed to her as if that would remedy the situation of having no birthday or Christmas present. Could the reason he had done it, to have impress her mom?

Knowing what she knew now, she was sure that had been the reason for the sudden chivalrous exploit. Who proposes to someone on their birthday when it was on Christmas Eve?

"Bah humbug. So be it." Mr. Rouge snapped his fingers, and everything became alive.

Her mom took off green oven mitts. Jacob moved closer to her younger self and put his arm around her waist as the conversation got underway. Talk of the weather and spending time at the beach was interrupted by a knock on the door.

"That must be Nick," her mom stated. "Remember him, sweetie, Nick Klaaws. He's alone this Christmas so I invited him over for dinner."

"Mom, no. I can't believe you did that. I told you I was bringing Jacob."

"I thought you might like more than just me to celebrate your birthday with tonight. I had already invited him. I couldn't very well have disinvited him, now, could I've?" A second knock sounded. "Go on, let him in. It's impolite to keep a guest waiting at the door."

Her mother had been right. An invite was an invite. She remembered being very upset. But viewing the situation now, she wondered if some unknown forces could have been working against her even then? Like pushing her toward Nick, instead of Jacob.

Mouthing "sorry" to Jacob, her younger self shrugged her shoulders. He gave her a smile, that at the time had melted her resolve. She'd been so in love with him. But now as she watched Jacob check his phone, an action she'd missed having gone to the door, led to how despicable he'd been. How could he propose to her and be in a relationship with another woman?

Refocusing her attention to the action at the door, her younger self said hello as she yanked the door open. Nick, the one person that had always been kind to her, no matter how rude she'd been to him, stood with an arm full of presents.

"Gloria?" He hesitated as a look a surprise crossed over his face, then disappeared. "No flat tire this time?"

Instantly, a tingling on her lips reminded her of their shared kiss on an off the beaten path road. It was as vivid as if it just happened. In her mind it had but for her younger self it had been years. Had he remembered it too?

Seeing a blush form on her younger self's cheeks, she wondered why she had reacted in that manner. She didn't remember having done so. For God's sake, she'd been almost engaged to the man she imagined to be in love with at the time. What did her blush mean? Why had it happened? She couldn't remember being embarrassed. No, that couldn't have been the reason. It had to been because she'd felt guilty. Their earlier kiss on a dark road, on her birthday, and how Nick had brought on suppressed emotions had nothing to do with her blushing.

"I—we flew this time and rented a car. Come on in."

"Your mother didn't mention you'd be here. I don't have a birthday gift for you this time. Unless—"

"Gloria, where are your manners, take those things from him. Nick, you're just in time to cut the ham."

The off handed slight hadn't gone unnoticed by her or Jacob, who had taken the arm full of gifts from Nick. Her younger self and Jacob shared a confused look.

Hearing the verbal exchange now, Gloria couldn't believe how rude her mom had been to Jacob. It was an added thing she'd have to look into when she returned to her time. It was time she shared the entire story concerning Jacob with her mother.

The three figures moved further into the kitchen and then froze.

Nick and Jacob stood next to each other. One with brown

hair and clean shaven and the other with black hair and a nine o'clock shadow. Nick was at least three inches taller and was definitely more muscular. Jacob appeared wimpy, in his usual attire, a dress shirt with a sweater draped over his shoulders.

It was preppy male versus natural male.

What had she seen in Jacob? Had it been the attention he'd given her while they worked together? Nick had tried to reach out to her several times, but she had refused all of his invitations.

Again, her stomach turned the more she studied Jacob. He'd used her. He'd been nothing at Marley & Associates, working in the accounting department, until they'd kicked off a sexual relationship.

It had been a chance meeting, or so she'd contemplated. She'd taken out a client while attending a conference, to eat and had run into Jacob. He had approached her as she was being seated and she had invited him to join them.

That night had been the kickoff of their relationship. He'd often walk by her office, stop in and chat. Their conversation had turned to restaurants they enjoyed, and then switched to business and her clients. The timeline of these memories triggered an outcry of emotions. The hurt from his betrayal still stung.

"Ms. White, love can be blind. Don't blame yourself," Mr. Rouge stated. He tugged her closer to the men. "Your questions are taking you a step in the right direction."

How could he be reading her mind? This whole dream was crazy. Why was she comparing Nick to Jacob? She and Nick had only shared a kiss on a dark road.

"I let go of my distrust of men when I embarked on a path to date Jacob. My father wasn't like him."

"Your father had problems, like I said earlier. He chose a different path, and it didn't include you. Jacob, on the other hand was simply a lost soul."

"And I fell for him."

"It was because of the path you chose to take. But the future is like a deck of cards. Your hand hasn't been dealt or defined yet."

Everything and everyone jerked into action again, and apprehension set in as she watched her mother, Nick, Jacob, and herself interact. They finished dinner with a high level of tension. No one demonstrated any joyfulness during the meal. The conversation was very minimal. It wasn't long after they had finished eating her mother cleared the table with Nick's help. Her younger self sat with Jacob like a king and queen being waited on.

When did I become so thoughtless?

As the last food item had been taken away, her mother ushered all of them into the living room. Nick took a seat close to the Christmas tree while her younger self and Jacob sat on the couch. Her mom placed a tray of cookies on the coffee table and remained standing.

"Let me give the first gift of the night," Jacob said. He stood and dug into his pants pocket, then knelt on one knee and held a solitary diamond ring. "Gloria, will you marry me?"

Viewing the proposal from this perspective it seemed fake, even staged. She hadn't had any warning, hadn't even considered the possibility of the question. Marriage hadn't been something she'd been ready to commit to yet. They'd only moved forward to dating after she'd gotten her big promotion six months prior.

How stupid she'd been. She'd played right into his

scheme, just when she'd been willing to let go of her bitterness aimed at men.

Nick, she saw sat stone still with his jaws clenched. Her mother was crying. Were they tears of joy, or of anger? She'd missed all the signs from the people who knew her the best. Why was everything so clear now?

CHAPTER
SEVEN
FOUR YEARS AGO - CHRISTMAS EVE: PART ONE

Once again, the creepy nothingness took over as Gloria struggled with regret. The last of the light showing the living room had dissipated. Rolling waves of panic gnawed at her sanity. A brittle silence stretched before her, and she clenched her hands together.

Etched into her mind was her mom's tearful eyes and Nick's crestfallen expression. A heaviness that was centered in her chest, led to a mass of disappointment in herself.

How could she have been so rude? No, so cruel.

From the depths of her memories, she unearthed an image of Nick as he left after Jacob's display of devotion. She had never deliberated on how it might have affected him until this moment. In all of the excitement of the proposal, she had missed his reaction.

She understood now.

Her disregard of the one person who was unfolding as a constant in her life and his feelings, hadn't been right on her part. Regrets of things she should have done assailed her like weights that were causing her to sink.

"No! I wanna go back," Gloria blurted out. "I want to see what Nick did."

"If you insist, but for the record, this is against the rules."

"Now there are rules? This is the craziest dream ever. There shouldn't be any rules."

The nothingness evaporated and she saw Nick standing by his truck looking toward her mom's house. She followed his gaze to the front window. The curtains hadn't been drawn and she saw herself staring out into the night. Even from this distant, her other self's facial expression was discernable. Her confused and sad look was something she didn't remember experiencing at the time. The happiness that should have been on her face wasn't there.

"Mr. Rouge—"

"Not now. Keep watching."

His stern tone, startled her. She opened her mouth, primed to question him, and then saw Jacob come into view. He put his arm around her and grinned.

Had that been deliberate? Aimed at Nick? She turned around to observe Nick. He gave a mocking hand salute to Jacob. Whom she now saw was nodding.

How could she have missed all this while standing next to Jacob?

"Damn him. I should have been the one asking Gloria to marry me."

Nick's statement stung.

"I'm sorry." She reached out to touch him, but Mr. Rouge pushed her closer to Nick. She whipped around, ready to give Mr. Rouge a thing or two for pushing her, but he had vanished. Not fully understanding her dream, she turned to Nick, who was still staring at her mom's house.

As if he'd heard her apology, his next words hurt even more.

"I'll wait for you. Today is just a technicality in the path of our future together. Gloria, you're my soulmate."

He used the side rail to climb into his truck and drove away.

Gloria wiped at a tear as it rolled downward on her cheek. "I've been so blind."

"Ms. White, it's best I get you back on track. I'm not here to judge you. We have to keep moving forward, remember. Time isn't on our side."

Refusing to look at him, she inhaled, hoping her out of control emotions would stop their erratic bouncing. "Where did you go?"

"I've been here the entire time to witness the things you should have seen."

"Oh really." Crossing her arms in front of her, she faced him. "It's all very convenient for you to mention time when YOU think it's time to leave. I thought you were controlling it."

He didn't answer. He simply stood in the middle of the street smiling at her. His blank look infuriated her. Why had her mind chosen him as the ghost or spirit pulling her through her failures?

"Whatever. Fine, what do you want me to see next?"

And just like that, the area became brighter. Squinting, she searched for Nick. Would she see him again?

Barely able to make out objects through the fogginess, she heard holiday music playing softly and doubted Nick would be in this induced memory. Because their paths hadn't crossed until today when she had needed a tow truck and fallen.

She was disoriented for a moment, as the area spun around her. Colors, shapes, and sounds merged together. She seized hold of Mr. Rouge's arm for stability. When the scene stopped spinning, a room with wood paneling came into focus.

Pivoting to her right, she saw more items, and gasped. One of the walls had a large three pane window that exposed a building across the street. Angling her body to the right, she saw a wall that held an array of modern art deco pictures.

Not just any artwork, but ones she'd helped Jacob pick for his office at the Marley & Associates Company. She blinked and then his familiar large brown desk became the focal point of the room.

Her legs became weak. A person was in the chair behind the desk that was facing the windows. It had to be Jacob.

A flutter of anxiety spurted through her. The mixture of anticipation and dread knotted in her stomach. If she followed the timeline that Mr. Rouge was showing her, then this was the Christmas Eve, she'd discovered that Jacob had been cheating.

"I'm done here," she said through her clenched jaw and squeezed Mr. Rouge's arm. "I don't need to relive this part of my life. It was painful enough the first time. No need to see it a second time."

Mr. Rouge peeled her hands off his arm and waved his hand. "Everything I show you is important. You've never seen it from this view before. A different angle always makes things clearer. Come, let's get up close and personal with your fiancé."

"My Ex!"

Gloria closed her eyes for a moment and the background

music stopped. Worst birthday ever. This one replaced that spot from when her dad had walked out. She'd been trying to erase it from her life for the last four years.

Lifting her head high, she opened her eyes. The music switched on again and Mr. Rouge led her around the desk to face Jacob, the two-timing asshole, who'd single handedly caused her disillusion of true love. It hadn't been her dad, like she told people. Jacob had been the person who had.

Allowing someone into her life had been a big step. After his proposal, she'd disregarded little warning signs, telling herself she just had to trust men.

The closer they stepped toward the chair the more she resisted. Then she saw him sitting with his feet up on the window ledge. His demeanor was that of a person who didn't have a care in the world. It was his smugness that she'd overlooked as vanity.

He was holding his iPhone to his ear not the office phone. A rush of contempt surged through her, as she looked at the man who'd broken her heart.

No, he hadn't. He had broken her spirit.

The feelings she had felt for Jacob had been artificial. Fake. They had fringed on the edge of wanting to love him, since he had declared his love for her. Gloria fully comprehended now, she had never loved Jacob. He couldn't have broken her heart, because she had never given it to him.

Her forehead creased as she tried to piece together what she just realized. If the two men she'd been blaming all these years weren't responsible, then why was she still alone?

A knot rose in her throat. Jacob hadn't sent her heart pounding at any time in their relationship. They'd only been sharing business conversations and planning. Their engagement announcement had been exciting and empowering at the time which had masked her true feelings.

Had the accidental meeting at a sales conference, just after she'd gotten her big promotion to Advertising Executive, been that?

Or had it been planned?

Had Jacob been stalking her?

No, she had been played by a player.

So much for the fairy tale romance, she'd thought she had found. It had only been in her imagination. All of Jacob's flaws and their relationships shortcomings were coming to light now.

She had paid every time they'd eaten at the five-star restaurants. She'd booked their airfares on her credit card when they traveled. He had moved into her condo, and never paid rent or had offered to.

Their long engagement now articulated more sense. No wonder they had never gotten around to setting a wedding date.

At the time, she'd never questioned the reason behind his hesitance to set a date. He had claimed their work schedules were too hectic to launch into planning a big wedding.

He had been right, of course. Their careers had exploded. Meetings, travel, and entertaining clients would have ruined the fun of being together. She had to admit, their conversations had been great. They would talk endlessly. No subject was off limits.

Gloria stared at him confused.

No, she'd done most of the speaking now that she thought about it.

"Sweetheart, someone might hear you."

Jacob's unforgettable deep voice brought her back to the scene in front of her.

"I have to pitch a new line of toys before I leave." He tapped his shoes together on the window ledge.

A new line of toys?

He hadn't ever presented anything to the board. Or for that matter, to her.

Unable to hear what the person on the other end of the phone was saying, but suddenly Jacob squirmed in his chair, closed his eyes, and smiled broadly. It softened his face as if he'd just yielded to the best sex ever in his life as he grabbed his groin.

"Behave," he snickered, let out a long audible breath and added. "I'll see you in the morning. We'll have an extra special Christmas morning delight when I arrive."

Who was he talking to? It hadn't been her, because they'd never had morning sex, he didn't like to. Or so he had said.

A conscious awareness sank into her mind. The full understanding of his deceit came full circle. First, his infidelity with her secretary. Second, all the lies. And third, his dishonesty.

She had shared a new design of a toy with Jacob the day before this. He'd been excited, saying it would be a game changer for the company. But he had persuaded her to wait until the spring line meeting to discuss it.

That meeting never happened. She'd quit and been forced to leave all her design portfolios on the company computer. The following year, the toy she had designed, was released by Marley & Associates and had been an enormous success.

Now she knew who had profited.

Jacob.

Could she sue them for theft? Or would it be her word against his?

"I want you to wear the nightgown I got you. I can't wait to see you in it."

Her anger rose a notch. Is this what Mr. Rouge wanted her to see, just how unfaithful Jacob had been?

The office door open and in walked yet one more version of herself.

Her hair was shorter and instead of the reddish highlights there was blonde. With her hands on her hips and creases on her forehead she stopped in front of the desk. "Jacob, are you ready to go?"

From her and Mr. Rouge's vantage point, she was able to see Jacob cup the end of the phone and whisper, "love you too." Her other self hadn't been able to see it because he had been facing the window. A shudder of humiliation coursed through her. The knowledge of his cheating was insulting.

Rage like she'd never experienced took over. Her palms were sweating, and a trapped feeling overcame her. Gloria tried to release Mr. Rouge's hand, but he held tight to hers.

The only person he could've been talking to, was his girlfriend, her secretary. She'd kicked him out of their—her condo soon after they had gone home this night. It was all too clear now as she watched the scene play out. How naive she'd been.

Jacob spun the chair around and slapped his hands on the desk. "Right. Hi, Sweetheart. I'll be only a minute more."

What a scum bag. Using the same name for both of them. The hurt altered into shame. How had she not seen he'd been cheating on her sooner? All the signs had been there. Late nights at the office, unexpected business trips, and of course all the text messages he'd been receiving.

"I'm so excited. Do I get my birthday gift now?" The past version of herself, sexily leaned over the desk ready to kiss him. His slight of not kissing her went ignored when he turned and reached into his pants pocket for his cell that had chirped, signaling he'd received a text message.

"Birthday gift..."

He didn't finish his sentence. From her angle with Mr. Rouge's help, she could see the message. A picture of her secretary, dressed in a sexy Mrs. Santa Claus negligee appeared.

Damn it. The depth of his lying was appalling.

"Sorry, last minute business. What did you say?"

"Oh, its fine. Everyone is trying to leave early for the holiday. Do you have my birthday gift? It's late in the day."

"Right, your birthday—"

"Stop it. Don't tease me. You've always given it to me early in the day, so to not ruin Christmas Eve." Her younger self walked around the desk and stopped in front of him with her arms crossed over her chest.

The scene changed again. This time they were inside her Boston condo. A tall real evergreen tree stood next to the floor to ceiling window. The entire living room was decked out in Christmas stuff. And that's what it had been. No rhyme or reason to any of the things. The condo had been staged for entertaining, not for meaning.

It was a part of her life she wasn't proud of.

With all of her promotions and Jacob's sudden interest in her, she'd fallen into the hype of a socialite. The elaborate decorating and overly priced furniture were all part of the picture she—no he—wanted to paint. She had allowed him to move in with her and let him brag to business associates the location of his residence.

It should have been a sign, but she'd overlooked it too. The fact was he had been the social climber in the company. She'd opened doors for Jacob, and he'd passed her by, leaving her in the dust.

Anger laden voices interrupted her reflection of her past. Two figures walked through the front door of the condo.

"I can't believe this! After all these years you simply forget it's my birthday today, Christmas Eve." Her younger self tossed her purse on the floor and threw off her coat.

"Listen Gloria, I'm sorry. I'll arrange a special getaway this weekend for us. We can order room service and a bottle of your favorite wine." Jacob moved closer to her younger self and put his hands on her arms.

"Don't touch me," she swiped at his hands and took off her boots. "You know how important it is to me to keep my birthday separate. You really don't have a present?"

"I ran out of time today." He discarded his outercoat and followed her into the kitchen. "Let's not fight. I said I was sorry. I'm taking a shower. Maybe we can have dessert before dinner. Why don't you join me?"

"Whatever. I'll start dinner."

Now that she could see his reactions to her anger, she wondered why she hadn't caught it before. Why would he have to take a shower when they had gotten home and before dinner? He never did that. Then it hit her. He must have spent his lunch time with his girlfriend and that was why he hadn't picked up a birthday gift.

She watched her younger self angrily pull items from the refrigerator and then stop when Jacob's phone began chirping and chirping.

Don't do it.

If she could warn her younger self maybe the hurt wouldn't be as bad. "Don't look at his phone."

"That won't work, Ms. White. You can't interfere with the past. What has happened will happen."

Bowing her head, she couldn't watch her younger self retrieve the phone from his coat.

"Please, Mr. Rouge, take me away. I don't want to relive this humiliation."

"Ms. White, it's not time yet."

Before Gloria could protest anymore, together they moved toward her younger self, who now held the phone. With a glance in the direction of their bedroom, she tapped the phone. A message and a picture appeared.

"Come over now. I'm ready to give you my Christmas present."

The photo was of her secretary, his girlfriend seductively laying on a bed wearing only a red and white lace Mrs. Santa Claus undergarments.

The pain she had felt at that one time, hit her. It crushed her insides, just like in the fifth-grade, the hurt of loving someone who didn't love you.

Would she ever find true love?

CHAPTER
EIGHT

FOUR YEARS AGO - CHRISTMAS EVE:
PART TWO

This jump to a different place left Gloria drained. The isolation of the blackness cooled her anger and hurt.

"I'm sorry you had to go through all that nasty stuff with Jacob," Mr. Rouge said.

She felt him near and reached out to him. "Saying sorry after the fact doesn't work for me."

"Perhaps, this will ease your pain."

The area around them became brighter. She could make out one person at the counter. Then a second person entered through a door, and they spoke.

"Mrs. White, nice to see you. How has Gloria been?"

"She's fine. She calls every once in a while. Too busy you know."

"Right, her big executive job and fiancé," Nick said.

Setting a large plate on a counter her mom continued, "I baked some of your favorite peanut butter kisses and sugar cookies."

"You shouldn't have, but I'm not going to refuse them.

Thanks for bringing your amazing Christmas cookies for me and the crew."

Her mom and Nick froze in place. Where was this?

"I don't recall ever being here, Mr. Rouge. How could I-we be here if I was never a part of this scene?"

"You did say you wanted to see Nick. This is your chance. Your previous choices did have effects on other people."

"Now you want to show me things. I can see that is my mom and that is Nick behind the counter. Your ability to let me be a part of things I wasn't aware of, or places I've never been to, seems a little suspicious."

Mr. Rogue shrugged his shoulders. "Let's say this is my gift to you."

"Fine. I'm not a gambler, but let's begin this new chapter."

She took a closer look around. It was very clear the two-timing Jacob wouldn't be anywhere in the picture here. Gloria wiped the last remaining tears from her eyes and promised that would be the last time she shed any for him. She inhaled deeply to free her mind.

Her new surroundings were that of a simple business reception area with a few chairs, vending machines, and a television. One wall had windows that looked out to a parking lot and the other two walls had car signs on them, advertising the brand names of vehicles.

This had to be the automotive repair shop her mom had mentioned bringing her car in to for service. Then she saw a banner hanging on the wall behind Nick that read, "NK TOWING".

NK? Did it stand for Nick Klaaws? Could he be the owner?

"Does that surprise you, Ms. White? You never gave him

a chance. You were so concentrated on only your run for fame."

Mr. Rouge's interruption of her thoughts hit a cord of dislike inside her. Apparently, privacy didn't exist in dreams. "Fame? I worked hard to become respected."

"That's what drove you, respect?"

"Yes. Women get the shit jobs. No equal pay. We are treated as inferior in the corporate world. Jacob capitalized on that, and I got screwed when we ended our relationship."

"My dear, when did Nick treat you as an inferior person, or do any of those things to you?"

Gloria glanced at her mom and then stared at Nick. He looked the same from the last scene with maybe a few more lines around his eyes, from having to squint in the Florida sunshine. "That's because I wasn't a threat to his job or business."

"Oh, I see," Mr. Rouge said. "If that's what you believe. Let's watch more."

Not waiting for her to reply, which was okay in her book because she didn't have a sassy comeback. Then, she heard her mom continue to talk.

"—you know I love to bake. I can't help myself during the holiday, but for heaven's sake I can't eat them all. Just being a good Samaritan." Her mom paused, and her smile faded. "Gloria hasn't been home for Christmas since— oh, excuse my chatter."

Gloria frowned. Had she neglected her mom? That can't be right, she had returned home after the doomed proposal. But the harder she searched her memories none came to her. She hadn't been home. Not once.

"Oh Mom, I'm sorry. I'll fix things."

"She can't hear you. Sometimes we are blind to the

obvious."

Closing her eyes, Gloria pressed her lips together as her anger rose. He was right. She had been so blind for so long. She had ignored the people who should have meant the most to her. "So be it, Mr. Rouge. I see now that I've hurt people I love."

"There is still hope for you, Ms. White."

She opened her eyes and heard Nick's sweet deep laughter. It sent delightful shivers down her spine.

"Whenever you want to share your incredible cookies or other dishes, just bring them on over, Mrs. White. The guys and me will devour them in a heartbeat."

"Woffff. Wooofff."

"Stop, Belle," Nick reprimanded a golden retriever by holding up a finger. The dog had come barreling around the corner, paying no attention to her master, and stopped in front of her mom.

"Oh Sweetie, I didn't forget you." Her mom knelt and rubbed behind Belle's ears. "Nick, there is a small sack of homemade doggie treats for her too. How old is she now?"

Belle moved away from her mom and stopped in front of her and Mr. Rouge wagging her tail. Gloria wondered if the dog could see them.

"Four. I got her Christmas Day—"

"That's right. I'm so sorry. If I had known that boyfriend of hers was intending to propose, I wouldn't have invited you over for dinner."

"I understand," he said and opened the protective covering on the cookies. "What are you looking at, Belle? Come here. Mrs. White brought you a treat."

That did the trick, Belle barked once and then ran to Nick, who was holding a doggie biscuit. "It wasn't your fault. Love has a weird way of working itself out. She'll always be the only one for me."

Her mom walked around the counter and hugged Nick. "You would've been a wonderful son-in-law."

"Nick! We need your help."

They broke apart as a loud male voice yelled.

"Thanks, Mrs. White. There is still time." He laughed and added, "They haven't set a date yet, have they?"

"Right you are. I haven't pressed the issue with Gloria either. I'll keep my fingers crossed for you."

"Nick! Where are you? We need you." The same male voice from before yelled.

"Be right there," he shouted and turned to face her mom. "Sorry to cut our time short, Mrs. White."

"No problem. I wanted to invite you and Belle over for Christmas Day dinner tomorrow. That is if you're available."

"I'll—we'll be there. Thanks again for the cookies."

The scene darkened and a bright light flashed.

Once Gloria was able to see, she saw her mom sitting next to a Christmas tree holding a picture. Not able to make out who it was, she leaned forward, squinting. That worked. Her mom was holding the picture of her, in her college graduation gown.

When was this? Her mom's house didn't give her an inkling since it hadn't changed in over twenty years. The couch and everything in the living room was the same as it was when she'd lived there.

"Oh Sweetie, I miss you. I wish you were here to celebrate your birthday."

Her mom's voice sounded strained. As if she'd been crying. Then on cue the house phone rang. Her mom got to her feet from the couch and picked up the receiver. "Hello?"

"Mom, I'm coming home. I kicked Jacob out. My flight doesn't leave until tomorrow afternoon."

"Oh my. Good thing I baked lots of cookies. I think we'll need them. I can whip up a birthday cake too."

How she was able to hear both sides of the conversation she didn't know. One look at Mr. Rouge and he shrugged his shoulders for a second time. Again, she heard her voice from the other end of the phone.

"No, my birthday is over. I can only stay for a few days. Oh Mom..."

Gloria pursed her lips. This was hours after the previous scene with Jacob. The phone call she just heard had been the hardest one she ever had to make. Admitting to her mom that the man she said she loved didn't love her, hurt. Facing the fact that her mom had been right, gave her the heebie-jeebies.

After she'd intercepted the lewd message from Jacob's lover, she had gone straight into the bathroom and threw his phone at him. It had crashed to the floor, breaking.

Jacob had tried to lie, saying he didn't know what she was talking about. At some point, during their argument he finally admitted to the affair. It hadn't mattered, the evidence on the phone was all she needed as proof. She allowed him the dignity of dressing. While he did, she stuffed his remaining clothes into trash bags, shoving them out into the outer hall. In a matter of an hour, all his personal things had been cleansed from her home. And his key laid on the kitchen counter, like a token of disregard.

The rest of the night was vague.

"If you'd like, I can take you back to that night," Mr. Rouge said.

Gloria blinked and shook her head. "No. I've moved on.

Even seeing him in my memories is bad. I don't want to see his face ever again."

More bright lights flashed and she—they were standing in front of her mom's house in Pelican Cove subdivision. The front door opened and Nick with Belle on a leash, came out. She then saw his company's tow trucked parked in the driveway.

She tilted her head. If she followed the timeline, this was Christmas Day, and she should be there at the house with mom crying her eyes out.

"Thanks, Mrs. White the dinner was excellent."

"Do you have to leave? Gloria should be here soon."

"That's why I have to leave. If she brought an end to her relationship with her fiancé, I'm the last person she'll want to see. Besides, she needs the comfort only you can give her. Maybe I'll see her around the area."

Her mom reached up and patted his cheek. "You make that happen. You hear me. She'll need you too."

"I can't make things happen. They just have to fall into place. Night, Mrs. White." Nick hugged her mom. "Come on, Belle. Time to see what Santa left you under the tree."

As his truck pulled away, a car drew near, and proceeded to turn into the driveway. It was her. They'd almost had a chance encounter. Why had fate been so cruel, by minutes?

"It wasn't meant to be. Fate wasn't on your side yet. It wasn't time," Mr. Rouge said.

"You and your god damn time. I'm sick of this. I get it. Nick has been there, and I haven't given him a chance. But the big question is why hasn't fate allowed us to have a relationship if, the stars say we are to?"

"Fate is, just what it is, fate. It can't be forced. Only embraced," Mr. Rouge stated.

CHAPTER
NINE
7:04 P.M. PRESENT DAY, CHRISTMAS EVE

B efore Gloria was able to untangle Mr. Rouge's riddles, the setting around her changed, and a thickness of shadows engulfed them.

Why hadn't Mr. Rouge shown her and her mom discussing Jacob's cheating while they sat on the couch drinking eggnog? They'd spent hours sifting through all the details. No, she corrected her thoughts. She had reiterated all the signs she had missed over the years of their engagement, while her mom had listened. It had been a one-sided conversation.

"You didn't have to take me to that time. First my dad and then Jacob, that's why I don't trust men. Seeing the heartache and feeling the pain, confirms my decision. No, I'm never falling in love, not even with Nick. Fate be damned. And I don't know why I'm talking to you. You're not real."

"Oh, I'm real, Ms. White. I'm here to show you love can be right in front of you. We all think affection is love when we meet someone we are attracted too. Love is special. But your soul is linked to another. You've been too blind to see it."

"Now you're impulsively bringing in the essences of souls. This is insane—I'm going insane. I'm done. Return me to my car or to my present."

Mr. Rouge took her hand. Light poles and palm trees took shapes from the shadows. More things emerged. Most noticeable was her parked car and the red tow truck.

A dejavu feeling came over her.

Her car had a few dents, and the tow truck was newer. The scene before could have been a replay of her twenty-second birthday, the night she'd gotten a flat tire.

"Thank you, Mr. Rouge." Gloria ignored the similarities; certain he'd had brought her back to her reality. Somehow her nightmare had come to an end. Trying to dislodge her hand from his, but she couldn't, Mr. Rouge held tight to hers.

"Let me go," Gloria yelled and tried again to pull her hand free.

"Oh no, we are here to observe," he crackled. "Look."

The silence broke, and night noises vibrated everywhere. Turning in the direction he pointed, there she was, motionless lying on the pavement in Nick's arms. It was as if she'd never left.

Her excitement of being in her time drained away. Why was she still viewing the scene if this was her reality? Why wasn't she in her body?

Mr. Rouge dragged her toward Nick and her other self. Closing her eyes, the sounds ended. They stopped in midstride. Her composed relief that she hadn't died vanished, and tears threatened to fall. What was the meaning behind dying on her thirty-fifth birthday?

"Ms. White open your eyes."

"No. I know this is an out of the body experience. I don't want to see my dead body. Just let me pass over to the other side. I can't take anymore."

"I've told you before, you are very much alive," he whispered. "I can only tell the truth."

None of this made sense then. How could she see herself in Nick's arms? She must have lost consciousness and her imagination was working overtime. It was playing havoc in her mind. As she tried to push through the powers of creativity, the question she had to reason through was how could Mr. Rouge, who wasn't and was her boss, been able to take her to specific moments of her past all involving Nick?

More important was why?

She continued to ponder these questions, but no explanations came to her.

However, she was willing to admit she'd been thinking of Nick lately. As a matter of fact, it was puzzling. The times he came to mind were whenever Mr. Rouge brought in fresh cut roses to display by the cash register. And she'd even contemplated trying to reconnect or call him. But never acted in case he'd gotten married. No telling how awkward that moment would have been.

Could that be the whole basis of this dream? Nick was her unfinished business. Books say when a person's dreams are pertaining to a relationship, that person has unresolved issues. But how could that be? Nick and she had only shared a kiss, or maybe a few. It had been a very passionate one, that had sent tingles through her body.

"Ms. White, your destiny is waiting."

The ghost Mr. Rouge's statement brought her to the matter at hand. "Fine, I'll open my eyes if you promise this is the last time, you'll show me what I missed."

"The past is the past, Ms. White. Your future awaits."

It wasn't the agreement she had hoped for, but at least it was a step in the right direction to end this ridiculous dream. Opening her eyes, she looked at Mr. Rouge who was smiling. Having never bargained with a ghost or an entity before, she wondered if she had just been duped. About to question him further, Nick's voice carried over to her.

"Hold on, I'm calling for help, Gloria."

She focused in on Nick and her limp self in his arms. The pain she heard in his tone pierced her heart. His concern for her wellbeing was transparent. He brushed wisps of her hair from her face and kissed her forehead.

Closing her eyes to halt the scene, she played out what she remembered. She'd fallen, hit her head on the parking lot pavement, and the tow truck driver had been Nick, who'd rushed to her aid.

So, how much time had passed?

From what she had seen, maybe only a minute or a few minutes. They were approximately in the same position before she'd lost consciousness.

Why had Nick said help was on the way? Was she bleeding? Had she broken a foot, a leg, or arm?

Panicking, she touched both arms and legs while keeping her eyes closed. She didn't feel any pain. The only thing that should have been hurting would be her head. But she'd felt it earlier and hadn't located a bump.

"Mr. Rouge tell me why I'm here with you instead of in my body."

"So many questions, Ms. White. This is what is going on now. Stop thinking so hard, just watch."

"You're twisting my words." Huffing, she shook her head and snapped open her eyes.

"Gloria," Nick yelled. "Answer me. Don't you die on me now that I've found you again."

Everything around them stilled. No wind. No sounds.

"Did you hear him?" Mr. Rouge asked.

"Find me again? Is that the part you wanted me to hear?" She tried to tug her hand free for a third time, thinking if she was able to, then the night dream would end.

"Has it forced you to do any reflections on your past?"

"Really? Now you want me to reflect. I'm clearly hurt lying there. I need help and you want me to scrutinize my past. This is stupid." Her voice rose and his hand tightened on hers.

"Think, Ms. White. What have I been showing you?"

"My past. Is this because I've died?"

He didn't say a word.

"Your silence must be your answer since you have to tell the truth. You've confirmed that I've died."

His continued quietness had her convinced she had either died or was nearing death's door. Everything she had been seeing could only be her subconscious mind replaying her life before her last breath. But why had Nick been such a big part of her memory, when in life he hadn't?

Blinking, she tried to force the scene to move. But it wouldn't. Her body lay in Nick's arms unmoving.

"Why won't they move?"

"It won't work. You haven't lived beyond this moment. Let's take an alternative journey. To some possibilities your life could have taken or could."

Unexpectedly, he released her hand. She stumbled backward as an eerie blackness besieged them. Before it fully engulfed them her heart raced, and she found it hard to breathe.

Had she been right all along, and she was dead?

As the last little bit of light disappeared, the last thought that echoed in her head was she'd died.

I'm dead.

I'm dead.

CHAPTER
TEN
THREE YEARS IN THE FUTURE - CHRISTMAS EVE

"**B**irthday Girl, wake up."

A deep masculine voice whispered near her ear, and then warm lips were pressing against her mouth, sending shivers through her. The doom of her death, that she was sure had happened, didn't feel like a cold and dark place. Grappling with the warm sensual mouth on hers and the earlier imminent destiny, Gloria opened her eyes.

The artful mouth ceased its sweet torment, and the man raised his head. It wasn't who she expected, as she found herself looking into a pair of blue eyes that belonged to Nick.

Is this the afterlife?

Where was Mr. Rouge? What was she doing laying instead of standing? More important was, how was she able to feel Nick's kiss?

"I have a huge day planned before we celebrate Christmas Eve. Get up."

Gloria blinked, but he was still leaning over her, shirtless no less. His well-muscled shoulders and chest were inches from her. Droplets of water from his wet hair fell on her face.

"Okay, give me a minute."

Nick laughed. "Since when does it take you only a minute for you to dress? I've had to wait up to an hour sometimes. Not that I'm complaining. I'll always wait for you."

He gave her an added kiss and disappeared into what she guessed was the bathroom. She sat upright and took in her surroundings, while fingering the quilt that covered her. It's bright red background with a mixture of Christmas trees and wreath designs clashed with the light blue curtains that hung over two large bay windows.

What the hell?

Never in her life would she have decorated her bedroom, or any bedroom like this. Christmas stuff belonged in the kitchen and family rooms, period.

Swinging her feet off the bed, she stood and realized she was naked. Preparing to take the ugly Christmas quilt from the bed, she saw a fluffy green robe laying on a nearby chair. Quickly, pulling it on, she tied the sash.

Ugg. Not my color either.

She turned in a full circle, but she wasn't able to get her bearings. Running a hand through her hair didn't help either. Her surroundings gave her no clues as to where she was or for that matter, when.

"Ms. White."

Gloria twisted around, ready to give Mr. Rouge a piece of her mind. He had promised not to show her anything from her past. But this couldn't be her past, this wasn't her bedroom or any she had been in.

Not able to find him, she glanced toward the closed door Nick had gone into. He'd said happy birthday, which could only mean this was December twenty-fourth.

But what year? The whole timeframe thing was wrong.

"Mr. Rouge?" She searched the room, but he wasn't anywhere. "Where are you? Why can't I see you?"

Still nothing from him. In a state of exasperation of being transferred into moments of her life, the need to escape this scene controlled her.

"I'll show you, Mr. Rouge, who is in charge. You can't manipulate me anymore." Taking small and slow defiant steps, she managed to quietly reach the only other door in the room.

"I wouldn't go out there yet. We still need to talk."

She stopped in mid-stride. "Now you respond."

"You're going in the wrong direction. That's the only reason I'm able to communicate with you. This is a picture of what your future could be," Mr. Rouge stated. "I'm not allowed in the unknown. Take a good look around you. This is a possibility."

"So, you're in my head?"

"Yes."

"I knew it. None of this is real," Gloria whispered and crossed her arms over her chest. "I've been dreaming. I wanna wake up now."

"You are awake. You have been the entire time. We can't stop yet. My job is to show you this future. Focus, Ms. White."

"Shouldn't I get a different ghost? In the Christmas Carol, there are three. I demand someone new."

Mr. Rouge's chuckle vibrated in her head. "You only get me. This is a sneak peek of three years into your future. It seems wonderful. You and Nick are together."

"Stop. We are not." Uncrossing her arms, she placed her hand on the doorknob, and rotated it to the right.

"Gloria, what are you doing? Your minute is up."

She turned.

Nick was coming out of the bathroom still wrapped in a towel around his waist. He walked toward her and banished the towel with a flick, sending it flying across the room. Forgetting to breathe, at the sight of his fully naked body, she inhaled sharply. Not only was his upper body well-muscled, so were his hips and thighs. Since she hadn't ever seen him naked, her imagination could never have done him justice. She lowered her eyes and briefly looked at his groin.

OMG.

He was perfect. In all ways a male should be. Unable to breathe, she held her breath, to calm her racing heart. She saw his bare feet in front of her. A spicy aroma that had to belong to his aftershave cologne besieged her senses. It was as if she knew or her body recognized the scent, when in fact she had never before smelled it. She closed her eyes as she raised her head, not wanting to see his passion filled face.

"Birthday girl, if being late isn't your intention, don't give me that sexy look."

Immediately, she opened her eyes hoping the scene had changed or stopped. But no, her worst nightmare was real. Nick was indeed standing in front of her naked. The base of his throat pulsed with his heartbeat.

Unexpected waves of longing hit her. It wasn't as if she'd never seen a man naked before, but this body belonged to Nick. The man who should have been her lover, according to Mr. Rouge and unseen forces.

His fingers gently touched her cheek, before his lips claimed hers again. Their sweet softness set off small fires through her. Gloria couldn't help herself and let her body melt against his. The warmth of his lips and body faded and she felt his breath on her ear. She sighed in anticipation of a pending kiss on her neck. Instead, he tugged the robe's tie and slid his warm hands over her hips. Bare skin touched bare skin.

"Stop teasing me, Mrs. Klaaws."

Mrs. Klaaws? I married him?

Her eyes widened. Nick's hands were roaming the swell of her back, causing the robe to expose her shoulders. Frozen in time, she didn't know what to do. This Nick was a stranger, but yet in this timeline he was her husband.

Then it happened. The robe fell to the floor. Fully naked, her body was responding to his as if this was an everyday occurrence. Gloria stared into his blue eyes that were darkened and filled with tenderness and were brimming with promises. Ones she didn't understand.

She imagined her next move and hesitantly released the door handle and took ownership to the fact they were naked. Placing her hand on his shoulder, his damp skin and the smell of an earthy clean fresh bodywash mixed with his aftershave intensified by the excitement of his nearness.

Nothing in her past relationships or with Jacob, had prepared her for this moment. It was so erotic. So enticing her whole body tingled, and a smoldering flame erupted.

Was this love?

If it was, this really was the first time she had experienced it.

"I'm all in for being late, Birthday Girl."

His hunger filled voice, was a soft caress, sending a new round of excitement through her. She released the breath she'd unknowingly been holding, and her common sense returned.

"I—I was going to go get a cup of coffee."

"Didn't you see it on the nightstand? I brewed one for you," he stated.

"Sorry, I didn't. Thank you."

"I've been planning this day for a while. Do you think I would have forgotten your morning coffee?"

Nick released her and she felt a sense of loss. Almost like a fire consuming all the air in the room. Still fully naked, he turned and walked to the nightstand and retrieved the cup. She tried to keep her composure and go with the flow as if this was an everyday occurrence of him standing nude in front of her.

Gloria forced her lips into a smile. "No, you wouldn't have. I must still be half asleep. Sorry, I'll go take a shower. That should wake me up."

Ignoring his outstretched hand with the coffee, she hurried into the bathroom. The door banged shut and she leaned against it.

This can't be real.

She looked at her hand and saw a gorgeous diamond ring and a thin gold band.

"I'm married. I'm Mrs. Klaaws."

"Stop acting like you're surprised at the use of your married name, Gloria."

Nick's words drifted in from the other side of the door.

Shit, she had said it aloud.

"I—um. I like hearing it." She raised her eyebrows, hoping that was the correct response to make. It must have been because he laughed.

"Mr. Rouge," she whispered.

When he didn't answer or appear, Gloria repeated his name in her mind.

"Yes, Ms. White, this is what could be. A life with a man who truly loves you."

"But how? I don't know him. We never dated."

"You do or could in the future. Three years have gone by since the night he came to your rescue. A lot could happen."

Gloria's forehead creased. Having a conversation with a ghost, in her head, while standing naked, was strange. How could this be her future?

That would mean she and Nick had dated and gotten married. Images of them at the beach watching the sunset and driving in a convertible car, flashed in a memory.

But how? They'd never done any of that. Grabbing a towel from the rack, she wrapped it around her. Ghost or not, he didn't get to see her nude. "I'm scared. Take me back."

"Are you sure? It sounds like the two of you are getting very friendly. Even to the point of engaging in—"

"Stop. The fact that you are listening and watching is creepy. What is going on here is private. Weren't you instructed on boundaries from the beyond?"

"I'm sorry. You're right. I crossed the line. We'll leave. I have one more timeline to share with you"

"No—no more. I'm done."

"What did you say, honey? Do you want me to join you?"

Nick's suggestive question went unanswered as the area around her vanished.

CHAPTER
ELEVEN
FORTY YEARS IN THE FUTURE

ciness prickled Gloria's skin as Mr. Rouge moved her to the next possibility of her future. But a nagging clarity that being with Nick had seemed right wouldn't go away. The seconds, minutes, and hours merged into what ifs. She patted her body and found she was wearing clothes again.

What could Mr. Rouge possibly want to show her?

Her life with the dead-beat two-timing Jacob? Would she still be living in Boston, working as a president of some company? The dream job she'd always wanted?

That would be something she'd like to see.

Or she and Nick, with children and grandbabies, living in a beachside home on the Gulf of Mexico? A nagging image of how happy he had been, turned into a gush of loneliness. She was and had been alone for a while. Spending a lifetime with someone who loved her, and she loved, was a possibility that had merit.

Gloria bit her lip in attempt to make sure she was alive, still not believing Mr. Rouge. Patches of light in the distant were a welcoming distraction, but her subconscious clung to the last threads of her real reality. She prayed she'd remember how she had felt being with Nick.

"Are you ready to see what's instore for you?"

Like the last scene, Mr. Rouge wasn't present in his body, only in her head. "Yes. Can we hurry through this one?"

"That word isn't in my vocabulary. Enjoy the show."

So, she'd be on her own again. An approaching catastrophe hit her, as palm trees and a sidewalk materialized. Then a four-story brick building with a sign, "Our Time Assisted Living", hanging above a set of sliding glass doors formed.

She found herself, standing in the middle of a circler driveway, and she stared at the sign. Who did she know that would've been placed in a nursing home? Had she put her mom in there? If she had, what did it have to do with her?

"Go on. Go inside," Mr. Rouge's voice told her.

"I'm repeating my question, is this the last one?"

"My time is almost up."

"That's not an answer. You're very good at being evasive in your replies."

His chuckle gave her an instant headache. She pressed two fingers to a spot on her forehead. With hesitant steps, she walked through the unopened doors.

"Weird," she thought.

It was as if she was a ghost. Was she invisible too? Or would she be an actor, taking part in the scenes like the last one?

The air inside was thick and had an odd smell. She couldn't place the odor. Then it disappeared as she emerged into a carpeted reception and waiting area. A few older people were hanging Christmas decorations on a mid-size tree, along with staff dressed in red uniform scrubs.

"Ms. White, is there anyone we should add to your guest list? You don't have anyone on it yet."

"There might be—no, there isn't anyone."

Gloria swung her head to the left, and gasped. A much-much older version of herself with gray hair and a walking cane stood by a counter. The woman who had asked the question was wearing a blue nurse's uniform.

Closing her eyes, the scene stopped. She took a deep breath. "Where have you taken me now, Mr. Rouge?"

"To another likelihood."

"You wanted to show me myself as an old lady? Everyone gets old at some point. This is a waste of your precious time."

"Choices. Everyone has them. What they do, to make their future theirs is because of choices. A person's future has many paths. Some go unused. Many are used several times. And others disappear when an option is chosen, shutting out those paths."

"You're talking in riddles. I'm tired, Mr. Rouge. That was a nice speech, but I don't have the patience to decipher the layers. The last possibility of my life we left was with Nick. Why aren't we together? Why am I alone?"

She hadn't opened her eyes, but sounds erupted around her, causing Gloria to open them. The nurse behind the counter was joined by a male and a second female who held a small cake and were singing, Happy Birthday. When the three finished, her older self still stood alone. None of the other residents had come over to join in the celebration.

Crap. It was her never ending birthday. Another version to experience again.

"Thank you for remembering. I've had way too many birthdays. They aren't special at my age."

"Oh, Ms. White, don't say that. No one should spend Christmas or their birthday alone. And everyone is special. Come on, I'll walk with you to your room so you can enjoy this wonderful looking chocolate cake."

One of the female nurses stepped around the counter and took a hold of her older self's arm. As the two disappeared around a corner, the other nurse said. "It's so sad when they get to this age, and they don't have anyone. They are the forgotten, to die alone too. I've seen it more often than I want to admit."

Alone?

Her interest rose a level wanting to see and hear more of this time period. Why didn't she have anyone? Had she outlived her family and friends? At her use of the word friends, Gloria cringed. Squeezing her eyes, she tried to picture at least one person she could recall as a friend.

No one came to mind. None of her school friends had stayed in touch with her as promised. Colleagues at Marley and Associates hadn't even called after she had broken off her engagement with Jacob, or when she had quit. Giving in to the realization she had no one during her golden years, sent an arc of sadness through her. Was she that bad of a person that no one cared if she was alive or dead? Why hadn't she taken more effort to stay in touch or make true friends? Mr. Rouge had said life encompassed all a person's choices.

Dismissing the scene in front of her, Gloria shrugged. It was what it was. She must have lived a good life.

"What is a good life worth, when at the end you're alone, Ms. White?"

"I'm not afraid of being alone. I must have had a good life. Look at this beautiful place, Mr. Rouge. If I could afford this, so what if no one came to my birthday. Maybe I outlived everyone."

"Taking the high road, are we?"

Before she could blink, he had whirled her away from the reception area and into a small room. A twin-size bed was pushed against a wall and a nightstand was next to it. An old and worn fabric chair sat next to another wall by a window. A small four drawer dresser stood adjacent to a second door, which could only be the bathroom.

"Is this the room of someone who's lived a happy and meaningful life?"

His voice screamed in her head again, and she flinched. Formulating a snappy reply in her head, she wasn't able to give it to him as her older self and the nurse walked in the room.

"I'll set the cake on your nightstand. Did you want a piece now?"

"No, I'll save it for later. Thank you."

"Oh, my, who is this young man in the picture with you?"

The nurse placed the cake on the nightstand and lifted a small, framed picture. From her position just inside the room she had caught a glimpse of who was in it.

Nick.

So, he had been in her life. The first female nurse at the counter had said Ms. White, not Mrs. Klaaws. What had happened to her and Nick?

"Just a boy I knew," her older-self replied.

Now why would she have called Nick a boy? That was a term you used for someone who was a pre-teen. Confused, she thought hard for a moment as the scene in front of her was put on pause.

"Mr. Rouge, this is wrong. I saw how happy Nick and I were."

She waited for what seemed an eternity for his one word reply. "Choices."

The scene moved again.

"He has a beautiful smile," the nurse said and replaced the picture on the nightstand. "What is he holding?"

"I don't remember. It was a very long time ago. I would like to be alone."

"Of course, Ms. White," the nurse answered. "You have a Merry Christmas tomorrow. I'll see you in a few days. I'm off for the holiday."

Her older-self ignored the nurse and stared off into nothingness, dismissing her.

Once the door shut, she watched herself break down and cry. Her olderself, lifted the picture and moved a finger over the image of Nick.

Gloria pursed her lips and choked on her own tears. The sadness in the room evoked a sense of desolation. Not a single item in the room screamed Christmas. Or struck any chords of personal items with memories. Why didn't she have a picture of her mom?

Hovering closer to the nightstand, she studied the picture, that her olderself now held. She couldn't place when it was taken, but Nick was holding a little white box.

It was clear he'd proposed. If he had, and she had rejected him, why would she have a picture of that exact moment? Mr. Rouge had said choices define a person's future. Is this her life if she doesn't marry Nick?

"That is correct. He's not in this future of yours. Your

paths never crossed after your very public dumping of Jacob. You stay on at Marley & Associates and became unkind, callous, and stingy with company's finances. However, the Nick from this timeline had asked you to marry him before you'd gone away to college."

"Are you saying the me I'm seeing has a life with no friends, no family, and no children?"

Mr. Rouge said nothing in her head, as she studied the still scene, and saw the sadness in her olderself's eyes.

"I'm not allowing this to happen to me. I understand the meaning of having people you love in your life. I promise to make changes in my life. I won't let Nick walk away from me —I won't walk away from him. I promise, Mr. Rouge. I promise—"

From somewhere the Christmas song, "I saw Mommy Kissing Santa Claus", played. The scene faded and a pounding in her head fired up into a full swing throbbing. Trying to hold on to the scene didn't work. When she opened her eyes, she was standing next to a grave. Only one person lingered next to the casket.

Nick.

His black hair was peppered with gray. It looked good on him, she thought. He stood tall with his hands clasped in front of him and his shoulders were still wide and only a few extra pounds around his middle.

When Nick lifted his head, she saw tears glistering in his still very blue eyes.

"Sir, excuse me, but we have to lower it," a man said as he approached Nick.

"Give me a few more minutes, please."

"Of course." The man and another man moved away as a tractor revved its engine off to the side.

Nick placed an age-old symbol of love, a single red rose on top of the casket. "Gloria, if the cosmos would've been on our side, you wouldn't have died alone. I will always love you for all eternity."

She didn't even feel her tears until she felt them rolling down her cheeks. Wiping at them, she continued to watch Nick. A sweet aroma surrounded her. How was it possible to smell the fragrance of the rose?

Why hadn't he fought for her?

The bigger question was how could she not have accepted his proposal?

He'd showed her he had been with her since fifth-grade, protecting her, being her friend, and giving her his love without her reciprocating it. He was truly her soulmate.

"I don't want this ending, Mr. Rouge. I know now Nick has been in front of me all these years and I've been blind— no, I've been insensitive. My behavior has been appalling. I won't let this happen. Please take me back. I know now I truly love him."

Nick and the casket faded into the emptiness. Thunderous sounds vibrated in her head.

"Ouch! Make it stop."

Gloria pressed her fingers to her temples as the emptiness and blackness took over.

CHAPTER
TWELVE
9:02 P.M. CHRISTMAS EVE, PRESENT DAY

"Gloria. Gloria, are you okay?"

From somewhere deep inside her, she knew the voice wasn't Mr. Rouge's. She felt strong arms cradling her close. Tentatively, she opened her eyes and found Nick staring at her.

How is this possible?

I am back in my own body?

She could smell his aftershave cologne, which brought forth a picture of her and him kissing in their bedroom naked. But they weren't there, they were on the ground in the mall parking lot. The nightmarish dreams had ended. She wasn't observing the scene with Mr. Rouge but living it. Lifting a hand to her forehead, she rested it there and shut her eyes to test her theory.

What if this was part of her weird dreams too?

Would she be able to hear the hum of the tow truck's engine or Nick's breathing, if she was still in the make-believe land? Unable to decide what was real or not, she reopened her eyes.

"Gloria? Why aren't you answering me?"

The concern in Nick's voice was also reflected on his face. Her heart sang with relief. She was in his arms. She was alive.

A new self-awareness coursed through her, and she grabbed a hold of his shirt. "Nick. Oh my God. You're not going to believe what has happened to me—"

"I do. You fell and hit your head. I was seconds away from calling 911."

"I know that, but I saw us together—we were..."

She let her explanation trail off when she saw his eyes widen. How did a person tell someone they'd had an out of the body experience? Or that she had seen them happily married? Mr. Rouge's repeated comment that she had to make choices came to her. This was the time to do it. A newfound inner strength gave her the power to do what was right.

"Kiss me, Nick."

His surprised look made her realize how odd her request had sounded. She'd lived a lifetime with him and one without him, but he hadn't yet. She laughed.

"I think I better take you to the hospital. You might have a concussion. You're not acting right."

Gloria used her arms to reposition and lifted herself from his grip. This forced him to release his hold on her. "I'm so sorry for how I've treated you in the past, Nick. But seeing you now, I know I've loved you all these years. I was just being stupid. So, get ready, I want to kiss you. Speak now if you don't want me to."

Cupping his face with her hands, she leaned in to show him she wanted him to kiss her. Her lips touched his firm ones, and she slid her hands from his cheeks, wrapping her arms around his neck. She kissed him deeper, and he matched the fever as if he didn't want it to end. After a few seconds, she felt one of his hands on her waist, and then the other on her back, pressing her closer.

He raised his mouth from hers for a moment and gazed into her eyes. "I've waited forever to hear you say those words. I love you too."

Before she could reply, his mouth captured hers. Locked into his drugging kisses time stopped. It was the two of them, on the ground, in the middle of a parking lot. She didn't care as it went on and on.

"Excuse me. Ms. White, is everything all right?"

She knew that voice. No! This can't be happening. This had to be her reality. This couldn't be part of the nightmare she'd gone through. Nick ended the kiss but held her tight against him and she refused to look at the holiday scrooge, Mr. Rouge.

"Ms. White, what is going on?"

Breaking away from Nick's gaze, Gloria looked beyond him and saw Mr. Rouge standing next to them.

"I could ask the same thing to you. What is going on?"

"Ms. White?"

"I don't tolerate lying. Why have you tricked me? You promised I could return to my time," she demanded and untangled herself from Nick's embrace and stood.

"Your time? I'm not sure I understand. Is there a problem with your timecard?"

His reply caught her off guard. The man in front of her was her boss, Mr. Rouge, minus his suitcoat, not the one from her imagination who'd been wearing jeans. "Um, no. I'm sorry. I didn't mean to be disrespectful. My car wouldn't—"

"Gloria fell and hit her head. I'm the tow truck driver, Nick, Nick Klaaws."

"And you, Sir, go around assaulting the women you help?"

Mr. Rouge took a step closer to Nick. She'd never seen this side of her boss before. The stern, well-dressed, man who was her boss, wasn't a champion to other people.

"Now listen here, whoever you are. I don't and have never assaulted a woman before," Nick declared and balled his hands into fists.

"Stop!"

Both men froze at her outburst and stared at her. She moved and took up a position in between the two of them. "Mr. Rouge, I'm off the clock so what I do isn't any of your business. But for the record, my car wouldn't start, and I called for a tow truck. When it arrived, I fell and Nick, who is an old friend, was here for me. Now you can tell me why you are here."

"I forgot to turn on the voicemail with our Holiday party info for tomorrow. I had to return to the store, and I saw your car and the tow truck."

"Okay then, that explains your presence," she articulated. "Now the two of you need to apologize to each other."

To her astonishment, her authoritative actions and voice had the desired effect on Mr. Rouge.

"I'm sorry sir. She—Ms. White is my employee. I was—Just checking to see if she needed any help. I shouldn't have jumped to conclusions."

"No problem. I understand. I'm glad she has someone looking out for her. Nice to meet you."

Gloria smiled as the man she loved held out his hand to

Mr. Rouge, who took it. They clasped hands in a mutual greeting.

"Nice to meet the man who has captured Ms. White's heart. She's kept you a secret."

She stiffened as her dream and the real time clashed. Some of her old insecurities pushed forward blocking her new resolve. "I'm still here. It's rude to talk about me in front of me."

The two of them laughed. Why would that be funny? She was confused at their actions.

"By the way Ms. White, I also forgot to give you your birthday card. I don't know what was wrong with me earlier. Excuse me while I go to retrieve it from my car." Mr. Rouge turned and walked away.

"He seems like a great boss," Nick whispered.

She threw back her shoulders and tilted her head. Mr. Rouge a great boss? In who's world? Not hers.

Then a nagging feeling that she had been judging Mr. Rouge, hit her. Just because he was a man didn't mean he was a bad person.

"Here you go," Mr. Rouge said and held out a white envelope when he returned.

"Thank you, but you didn't have to," she replied and took it.

"No one ever has to do anything. What counts is that someone is thinking of you."

Blinking, to see if the scene stopped or changed, she struggled with Mr. Rouge's comment. Ashamed for not taking in account that he too might be alone. Was he married? Did he have any children? Did he live close to the mall? Or did he have to drive miles? She couldn't answer any of her questions. It was time to change that.

"If you're not doing anything after the store's Christmas party, would you like to join me and my mother? She's a great cook. Nick can vouch for that. She's always making more then we can eat."

Mr. Rouge's surprised look said it all.

"Nick has agreed to join us too," she said, taking his hand into hers. "Aren't you?"

She couldn't help but smile. Here she was, on Christmas Eve, inviting not one but two men to her mom's for dinner, who would freak out for a moment. Then after a few seconds everything would be okay. Or would it?

"Ms. White, it's not proper company protocol, however, I would love to. Thank you."

"That's a checkmark in the yes column. Nick, are you in too? I know you love my mother's cooking?"

"Yes. You don't have to ask me twice."

"Good. It's settled. I'll see you both tomorrow," she stated and took a step toward her car and stopped. "Did we figure out what is wrong with my car?"

"Oh, right. I better finish the job here, birthday girl. Pop the hood," Nick said.

"And I better go change the voice mail message. Enjoy what's left of your special day."

"Thank you, I will." She tried to sound happy, but it sounded forced to her. What did she have a few hours left? Not much time to celebrate. Shifting from one foot to the other, she watched Mr. Rouge walk into the store, afraid he'd reappear to show her yet one more of her birthdays.

A roar of an engine, had her turning toward her car. Nick had applied jumper cables and was inside her car pressing the gas pedal. He smiled and nodded his head. Exiting her car, he began unhooking the cables.

"Just a dead battery. I would suggest buying a new one in the next week or so. Stop by my shop and I'll get it for you," he said and closed the hood of her car.

When he turned, she saw he had a smudge of grease on his cheek. It was so sexy, she sighed.

"What? Is something wrong?"

Raising her eyebrows, had he heard her? "Nothing. I recall a different night that you came to my rescue."

"You do, do you?"

"Yup, if my memory serves me right, it ended with a kiss."

He moved closer to her. "It did."

Expecting him to kiss her, she closed her eyes, but the kiss never came.

Shit. She reopened her eyes. Had she overstepped some unseen line?

"Gloria, I don't play games anymore. If you want me to kiss you, it won't stop there."

"Are you saying you want to have sex with me? I've never had anyone just come out and ask. But yes, I would love to."

"That's not what I mean. I don't just kiss women. When I do kiss a woman it's because I have feelings for her. Which by the way, hasn't happened in a long time and then there is the whole sex thing."

She filled the empty space and wiped at the grease mark on his cheek. "Nick, I want you. I want you in my life. I should never have pushed you aside. I still remember how you came to my aid in fifth-grade, after I made a fool of myself."

"You do?"

"Oh yeah. And our eighth-grade beach day. I still have

that bracelet you crafted for me."

"For real, you do?"

She slid her hands over his hard-rock chest. "My number is two-three-nine, seven-four-two, one-six-six-five. I know its seventeen years late, but I want you to call me."

Nick's eyes opened wider.

"Please believe me. I've seen the light. And I know you have been the one constant in my life. I was just—"

His mouth covered hers, cutting short her declaration. They kissed and clung to each other. Nothing else mattered. It was just the two of them. The joy of being in his arms was a dream. As if it was some long-awaited meeting.

An alarm sounded and Nick ended the searing kiss. "Sorry. I have to answer that, it's my ring tone for emergency calls."

"Can't you let it go to voicemail?" She sighed, wishing the moment would never end.

"Gloria, that would be rude. Like I said earlier, I'm on call tonight. I keep my promises. I will be at your mom's for dinner. But I do need to take this call."

Allowing him to step back, she smiled. "I understand."

"Hello, NK Towing." He turned away from her as he talked. The more she observed him the more she lost her heart to him. Nick was the kind of man who was concerned for his client's wellbeing, just as he had been for hers. Even his body language told her, he was a man of his word.

If, she saw all this now, why hadn't she on all the other occasions?

When he ended the call, he turned and gave her a smile. "Sorry, I have another stranded driver that needs my help."

"You're forgiven. Maybe we should continue where we left off."

"I'd love to, but I have to make sure your battery is charged enough."

"Oh, it is," she murmured. Even with the truck's headlights shining on them, she saw his eyebrows lift. "You meant my car's battery, not me."

He cleared his throat. "I'm glad both have been jumped started."

Laughing, she went to him and kissed him. "You better be prepared for when we have more time to be together. But you're right. Someone else needs your help and I have to rise early, and it isn't for Santa. I have to work the store's Christmas Event."

"What about what's left of your birthday? You have to work on Christmas Day?"

Again, her birthday. She grinned. "Not much left of it, is there? I'll have one next year and the following and so forth. No big deal. I do work tomorrow, but only for a few hours. It's the store's tradition, a customer appreciation giving party."

"All right," he said and took her hand. "I hope the rest of your birthday is as special as the last half hour has been."

"Nothing can beat this one. Although, there is one—I better get going." She couldn't say anything about their future together. It would be best to leave things in the moment and not dwell on the past or what could be.

Nick walked her to the driver's side and shut the door once she was inside. She lowered the window.

"The battery should be good until you can come to the shop for a new one in a day or so."

"Thanks again for always being there for me. I'll see you tomorrow."

He leaned in and kissed her. The moment his lips touched hers, her stomach flipflopped.

"Merry Birthday, Gloria."

"How do you know about that?"

"It was on your car bumper that night. I asked your mom. She told me it was her special way of saying Happy Birthday to you. I hope you don't mind I used it," he said.

"No, you can use it. Now it will mean more to me. Night, Nick." Her heart skipped a beat as she drove away. In a far off place somewhere in her mind, she wondered if time would stop, and this had all been only a possibility.

CHAPTER
THIRTEEN

G loria flung her hand toward the nightstand, hitting the alarm clock button.

"Whoever invented those damn things should be put in jail," she thought. Prying her eyes open, the red numbers on the clock showed it was five-thirty.

Time to get up and go to work.

Swinging her legs over the side of the bed, she hurried into the bathroom. But as she stood in front of the mirror, the memories of the weirdness of Mr. Rouge and Nick had her wondering if she had dreamt the whole thing. Her entire drive home last night had been in a haze of confusion.

How could she have gone into her past, or traveled back in time?

Or, gone into the future?

She shook her head and decided it had been a dream after she had blacked out for a moment from hitting her head. The only real things had been her car not working, Nick coming to her rescue once again and the kiss. It had been undeniably real, and she touched her lips that still felt a little swollen.

The alarm clock sounded for a second time, and she ran to her nightstand and turned it off, instead of pressing snooze again.

Five-forty-five.

Thank goodness for snooze buttons. Okay, she'd give credit to the inventor of that feature.

Retracing her steps to the bathroom, Gloria washed up, since she had taken a shower before going to bed. Dressing in a black pair of slacks and a white button-down shirt, she added a new holiday red sweater she'd bought with her discount. Pulling her hair to the left side she used a scrunchy to secure it in place. Satisfied she looked presentable and not like she'd lived in a lifetime in a few minutes, she left her house in Morning Sunshine subdivision.

The drive to the Starbucks for her a.m. shot of caffeine was short and the first sip of the Caramel Macchiato was heaven. The sweet caramel and the chocolate sent her taste buds into overdrive. By the time she arrived at the mall she'd finished the drink and wished she had ordered a Venti instead of only a Grande. As she parked her car, scenes of the night before rushed forward.

Nick had arrived in a tow truck with Christmas music blaring.

She fell and hit her head.

How she ended up laying in Nick's arms in the middle of the parking lot, she didn't know.

She smiled, remembering how it had felt being protected and comforted. She didn't want that feeling to ever go away. Nick was her future for sure.

Once outside of her car, she saw Mr. Rouge waiting at the store's door. She checked her phone for the time.

Six-fifty-one. She'd done it. On time and early.

"Good morning, Mr. Rouge."

"No car troubles this morning," he murmured and held open the door.

It wasn't a question; it was more of a statement. Not sure if he expected an answer but thought it would be appropriate for her to reply. She took a breath. "No, none."

"I hired a photographer. She should be arriving shortly. The caterers will be here in fifteen minutes. And Santa Claus is coming at nine-thirty for a big entrance."

He was all business like normal. The other Mr. Rouge, in her dreams, had been easier to talk too. "Should I fill the goodie bags?"

"Goodie bags? If you are referring to the gift bags, they are in the back room. I have everything laid out that I want to go in them. I'll process the gift cards and bring them to you. Remember to put in the postcard with the upcoming sale and discount. It's usually a huge success for us after Christmas."

For a moment Gloria wondered if she had really invited him over to her mom's. What if that had been in her dream too? Sending caution into the wind, she brushed aside her apprehensions. "One thing, before I stuff the gift bags, you are coming to my mother's for Christmas dinner, right?"

He stopped in mid-stride and turned to face her. "Yes."

The one-word reply sounded rehearsed. "Great. I have to ask a favor. I need to call her to let her know you are a yes. Would that be, okay?"

"If you must."

Without saying a single word, he walked away. His actions worked in her favor. She had forgotten to call her mom when she had gotten home last night. Stepping into the back room, Gloria pulled out her phone from her purse and hit "call mom".

"Honey, what's wrong?"

"Nothing. I don't have much time. I'm at work. I invited two people over for dinner tonight."

"I think there must be something wrong with the phone. I heard you say you invited not one, but two people over. For this evening."

"Yes, mom. Nick and my boss, Mr. Rouge. Gotta go. Love you."

Not allowing her mom to ask any more questions, Gloria tapped "end call". Taking a deep breath, glad that was over, she launched into stuffing the gift bags, not goodie bags with the items on the table.

It was a mindless task and her thoughts wandered. If she had dreamt everything, what was its meaning? Had she rushed into her declaration of love to Nick? Admitting she loved him, and then inviting him over to dinner was outright bold on her part.

Things were getting more complicated by the minute. Her goal to find out more about Mr. Rouge wasn't working either. His cold demeanor was holding her at bay of asking personal questions. They hadn't had any time for small talk this morning when she arrived.

How was she to break through the icy wall he had around himself? Or was she the one who'd been so unfriendly and cold?

"What on earth did I do?"

"Is something wrong, Miss White?"

Jumping a little, she turned. "No, Mr. Rouge. Just a paper cut."

She stuck her finger in her mouth, pretending to have gotten one, not realizing she had said something aloud. But there was something wrong. She had invited Nick and Mr.

Rouge to her mom's for dinner. It was definitely going to be very interesting.

"Here are the gift cards," he said and placed them on the counter. "Once you have inserted them, the gift bags should be good to go. The photographer is here. I'd like to introduce you to her when you come out."

"Yes, of course," Gloria said and scolded herself for daydreaming. She didn't want to get on Mr. Rouge's bad side today. Quickly slipping the gift cards into the bags, she took an arm full and went out to the sales floor.

"Here she is. Ms. White I'd like you to meet Ms. Londone."

Dropping a few of the bags at the mention of the name Londone, she set the rest of them on the top of a display fixture. As she turned, there in front of her was Donnette, her grade school friend. Gone was her long blonde hair and glasses. She looked like an adult version of the girl she had known.

Was fate tempting her with choices?

"Donnette?"

"Gloria?"

"Yes. Omg, you've been on my mind. As one of my New Year's resolutions, I was going to try and find you."

"Me too," Donnette replied and smiled. "I've missed our friendship—"

A loud clearing of a throat interrupted them. They both pivoted in unison to face Mr. Rouge.

"It's apparent the two of you know each other. How nice. There will be time later to reconnect. Ms. Londone, if you need anything Ms. White will assist you."

Gloria held in check a sarcastic reply and waited for him to walk away. When he did, she rushed over to Donnette, and they hugged. "Disregard his arrogance. It's all for show. How have you been?"

"Fantastic. My photography business has taken off since my art show last year in Naples. How have you been? Did you and Nick ever get together?"

Tilting her head to one side in confusion. "Me and Nick?"

"Yeah, he had such a crush on you for years. I was convinced that once he got the nerve to ask you out, it would turn into an ever after."

"No, we never—that is until—it's a long story," Gloria said and glanced in Mr. Rouge's direction. "I better get you set-up. What do you need?"

"Right, sorry," Donnette said and gathered up her tripod and camera. "I'm just so excited we found each other again. He—Mr. Rouge said he wants portraits of each of the guests with Santa. Let's assemble everything over by the front door and at that wonderful Christmas tree."

"That will make a nice backdrop."

In a matter of minutes, they had rearranged and placed chairs around the Christmas tree.

"Oh, by the way, Happy Belated Birthday."

Stunned, Gloria paused for a second before replying. "You remember my birthday after all these years?"

"Yes. I was so jealous that you had such a great day to call yours. But I hated we never got to celebrate your birthday on your birthday."

"That means so much to me, Donnette. For years I've tried to hide my birthday. I didn't like having to share it with the world. But that stops now. And I'm sorry I don't recall yours. That must mean I wasn't a very good friend. Was it August fifth or the third?"

Donnette laughed. "See, you do know when it is, August

third."

"Ms. White, are there more gift bags?"

She rolled her eyes, so only Donnette could see. "Yes, I'm on my way right now."

"Sorry I got you in trouble."

Giving her long lost friend a smile, Gloria went to the backroom to retrieve the remaining gift bags. With her arms full, she returned to the salesfloor, but collided into someone. Bags and gifts went flying.

"Miss White, are you alright?" It was Mr. Rouge who caught her arm and steadied her before she joined everything else on the floor.

"I am. Sorry, I didn't see you."

"No, it was my fault. Let me help you refill the gift bags."

He bent downward as she did, and they bumped heads.

"Ouch!"

She dropped all the remaining bags and lifted her hand to her head. "Really, I have this, Mr. Rouge. I am capable of doing my job. I don't need you to micromanage me. I have managed an entire department before. And I do have a first name. It's Gloria."

As the words she'd been holding back for months came out, the air around them glistened like a bright light had been turned on and then turned off.

Gloria quivered.

She looked around expecting to see the ghost Mr. Rouge to appear and take her back in time or to another possible future. But he didn't, the real Mr. Rouge, her boss, was standing in front of her.

"Ms. White, I'm sorry you feel that way. That was never my intention. I do know your first name. Sometimes I forget I don't have to be so formal."

Eyeing Mr. Rouge for a moment, to make sure it was her boss, she knew this was her time to speak up.

"Well, this is part of my New Year's resolution too," she took a deep breath and continued. "I'm good at my job if you'd only let me show you. I have some ideas on how to improve our sales at the cash register."

He cleared his throat. "I'll understand if you want to withdraw your invite to Christmas dinner tonight. However, the reason I followed you was to give you your bonus. And now that you hinted at ways to improve sales, I would love to discuss how you think that is possible."

She didn't hear anything he said but the one word, bonus.

"Now? Isn't the bonus usually on our paycheck? Are you firing me?"

"Goodness no. I just asked you to tell me your ideas. Why would you think I was firing you?"

How should she respond? Tell him that she thinks he hates her or take the high road. One of the lessons she learned from her Christmas Carol nightmare was to tell the truth.

"Where should I begin, Mr. Rouge? Let's see, you are always on my case about the stupidest things. You check my work time after time. I'm overqualified for this position, but it seems like I can't do anything right in your eyes."

"If that is how I've made you feel I'm sorry. I've seen your potential from the beginning. I guess my actions could have been taken in the wrong way. I have been taking measures to make sure you were approved for a promotion. The bonuses for regular employees are on their checks. But this year I have a special bonus for you. I felt it was time to make you Assistant Store Manager. And their bonuses are given out in a separate check, along with your pick of four pieces of clothing."

Gloria stood and she stared at him. "You're promoting me? To an Assistant Store Manager?"

"Yes, if you accept it. I wanted to talk to you before the photographer got here however, she arrived earlier than I expected. I'm sorry, this is not how I wanted to ask you or tell you."

"I don't know what to say. Thank you."

He stood too, reached inside his suit coat, and withdrew a white envelope. Gloria White was written on the front in very stylish letters. "You can sign the papers tomorrow when you come in."

She took the envelope and didn't know what to do with it. "I'll put it in my purse. And yes, you are still invited to my mother's. Thank you. I better get these gift bags refilled. Our guests should be arriving."

"Right you are. I'll leave this task in your very capable hands."

He left her then, holding the envelope and items scattered on the floor. What had just happened? She opened the envelope and gasped.

The bonus—no, her bonus amount was more then she earned in a month. Fate was definitely on her side now. She'd be able to pay some bills and then some.

In the distance, she heard Mr. Rouge greeting a customer and knew she'd better hurry. Collecting the scattered items, she placed them in the bags. Before going onto the sales floor, she put her bonus check in her purse.

Stretching her arms around the bags, she secured them and then returned to the front desk with a smile. The ghost Mr. Rouge had been right. Choices do make a difference.

CHAPTER
FOURTEEN

"Mom, stop worrying. Nick was very appreciative of the offer, and Mr. Rouge isn't royalty. He's— he is just my boss," Gloria stated as her mood became lighter. The thought of seeing Nick sent a flutter through her.

"I wish I had more notice. Your phone call this morning telling me you invited two people for dinner wasn't very considerate. If you were younger, I'd ground you."

Gloria laughed. "You never grounded me. Now you want to start?"

"It's not funny. Nick I'm okay with, he's been over plenty. Now your boss, is another story. I have never met him. You've mentioned how you don't like him. So, I'm at—was at a loss on why you would invite him. You know it's important to me that things are just right when I entertain."

Her smiled faded. Her mom was right, she didn't know Mr. Rouge well enough to be inviting him over for dinner. Had her dream ghost version of him compelled her see her boss version as just a man? Or someone with feelings and problems he could be going through in his own life?

To justify her late night decision of inviting Mr. Rouge over for Christmas dinner, she told herself it was because she had seen a different viewpoint of him. This morning at work he had been kind, understanding and given her a promotion. Which had been a surprise that she wasn't sure she wanted. It would involve working more closely with him and more responsibility. Time will tell if their truce was real. She wouldn't hold her breath on it.

Had she worked through all her stressful emotions? The ghost Mr. Rouge had shown her a new outlook on life. Gloria knew she was capable of being an assistant store manager, but did she want to do it?

Those were questions she would have to resolve soon, but now was not that time. Today was Christmas and guests would be arriving at any time. Refocusing, Gloria completed folding a white cloth napkin into a shape of a Christmas tree and mentally thanked Martha Stewart.

"Everything looks great, Mom. Don't worry. I'll finish up with the table, you go change," she said.

"Oh lord, look at the time. Right."

Her mom spoke in a rushed tone and smoothed her hair absently, a sign she was nervous. Gloria nudged her mom from the dining room. "Go."

That did the trick. She was alone at last.

Her mom's worrying had been thinning on her nerves since she'd arrived two hours ago. First it had been that there might not be enough food. Second, it was the lack of time. Thirdly, it had been her mom's non-stop talking. All she did was say how great Nick was, and how glad she was they'd finally reconnected. If calling for a tow-truck and literally falling into his arms was reconnecting, then fate was getting a bad rap.

What had her dream Mr. Rouge said? Fate is just what it is, fate.

Within minutes, she was going to find out when Nick arrived if fate was really real. The air around her stirred. Was that fate answering her? It had to have been. She felt a thread of excitement within her, but she pushed it away. It was too soon to tell if the bond between her and Nick would last.

To calm herself, Gloria focused on the plates, the folded napkins, and silverware making sure they were all set in place. A little Christmas tree crafted of poinsettia's along with reindeer were the only decorations in the middle.

Simple, but an effective look.

Her mom was the most creative person she knew. She could make grass and leaves into a masterpiece. Hence, her own ability to turn a square napkin into the now gorgeous tree decorating the dinner plates.

Sorry, Martha. You weren't here to do the work, I was.

Smiling, she walked from the dining room to the living room and then back to the kitchen, but it faded, and Gloria frowned. The nightmarish images she had envisioned after hitting her head, ran through her brain. More appeared and they with others became a recap on steroids. Pressing a finger to her temple and closing her eyes didn't help.

She saw herself getting off of work.

Finding her car had a dead battery.

Nick's passionate kiss.

Her heartbeat faster. The surprise of seeing him in person after all these years had struck her ardently in the gut. She'd always pushed any rising feelings for him deep into the never-never parts of her emotions. Until the remix scenes of her life with Mr. Rouge being the narrator, had opened her eyes allowing the suppressed feelings to come forward.

It, they, and them, still seemed like dreams or things she'd fabricated for some unknown reasons. She had been power-less to stop the visions from replaying all night and morning. The worst part was she still wasn't able to make heads or tails out of them. Or, why she'd been remembering her past so vividly. The only event, Gloria knew to be real was the one that happened after Nick had jumped her dead car battery.

Their kiss.

It had touched a part of her she hadn't thought possible. He hadn't been demanding or forceful with his lips, only searching. She had answered back with a need of wanting of her own.

If he hadn't received a new emergency call, she wondered what would have happened. All kinds of possibilities came to mind.

Would she have invited him over to her place? Would he have stayed?

Maybe, they'd would have gone to a 24/7 restaurant and sat for hours talking.

Or nothing. Only an awkwardness, and they would've said goodbye, promising to call each other.

"Honey, didn't you hear the doorbell? I think that's enough nuts in the bowl."

Gloria jerked her hand in surprise and looked down. Nuts were heaping over the sides of the bowl and scattered on the countertop. Then she heard the blink doorbell chime. "No, I didn't. Sorry mom."

"Clean up the mess quickly. I'll go let in our company."

She watched as her mom elegantly walked through the doorway in a pair of black pants, a short sleeve white lace shirt with a red beaded necklace which had added just a touch of color and hung low, swaying slightly. Her dark brown hair had been arranged into a ponytail with a decorative green scrunching. She wasn't sure why her mom had dressed in something so stylish, but decided it was good to see her this way. It was time her mom did.

From the kitchen she heard the front door open and close.

"Hello, Nick. Come on in. I'm so glad you were able to help Gloria last night."

"Merry Christmas, Mrs. White. I was just doing my job. I brought a special non-invitee with me. I hope that is okay."

"For heaven's sake, yes. She is always welcomed here. Gloria is in the kitchen."

The sound of paws clicking on the tile floor and then a woof, caused her to drop the plastic bowl of nuts on the floor. As she bent to clean them up, a golden colored dog just like the one she'd seen in Nick's shop in the dream, proceeded to lick her face.

"My, my is this how you greet everyone, Belle?" Gloria laughed.

"Girl, stop!"

Nick's command went unheeded by Belle, who continued to give her doggie kisses. Neither her mom nor Nick caught the fact that she'd called the dog by her name as they arrived on the chaotic scene. Adding to the confusion, the doorbell chimed. She hoped her miscue would go unnoticed.

"That should be your boss. Gloria, why haven't you finished cleaning?"

Unable to answer as Belle butted her head into her

AVOIDING MY MERRY BIRTHDAY

chest, causing her to fall backward. Nick was once again there to aid her. He tugged Belle away and knelt beside her. Gloria laughed so hard, she wiped tears from her eyes. Nick took Belle by the collar and held her off to the side.

"Gloria, are you okay?"

"Yes—yes, I am," and added, "She is a handful, isn't she?" As she scooped the fallen nuts into her hands, she looked at Nick. "I hope nuts aren't harmful to her. I saw her take a couple."

"They looked to be just peanuts, so it is all good. I'm sorry. Belle is usually very well behaved. I'm not sure what's gotten into her. It's like she knows you. But you and she haven't met."

His comment had her laughing again. They had met in her dream. Somehow Belle had known she had been in the shop that day watching. Indifferent to making any sense of it, she hugged Belle and whispered, "You and I are going to be best buddies."

As a reply, she received a tongue kiss. Gloria stood and dumped the fallen nuts into the trash can. But they almost went flying again when Belle barked as her mom and Mr. Rouge came into the kitchen.

Smiling, Gloria brushed her hands together, getting rid of the peanut dust. "Good evening, Mr. Rouge. We just had a little accident. You've met Nick, and this four-legged adorable dog is Belle. I hope my mother introduced herself, or do I need to formally do so?"

When neither, Mr. Rouge or her mom spoke, she noted their concerned looks and caught them glancing at each other weirdly.

"No, as a matter of fact, I have met your mother before it

seems," Mr. Rouge stated and inhaled deeply. "I should say, years ago."

The room went silent, even Belle found a spot next to the Christmas tree to lay. Tilting her head to the side, Gloria looked at Nick. He shrugged his shoulders.

She then stared at her mom. There was no smile on her mom's face, only a slight blush which added color to her cheeks. Having never seen her mom blush before, Gloria was confused. Mr. Rouge, who stood with his arms folded across his chest was smiling from ear to ear.

"Okay, either I'm dreaming again, or I have a concussion from last night. You two know each other?"

Her mom nodded and Mr. Rouge unfolded his arms and placed a hand on her mom's arm. "Yes. I didn't know Carol was your mother. She and I..."

"All this time. All the things we have been through, and you're telling me you didn't know until you came to the house that you knew my mom?"

"Yes. I never knew her married name. I never married, hoping someday I'd find her again. We had met at night school. We were design partners—"

"Oh, my goodness. You waited all these years? You've been on my mind often, Stan."

"Wait a minute," Gloria demanded as she eyed her mom and Mr. Rouge. "This—this can't be happening. I don't understand, mom. You went to night school? When?"

"Sweetie, it was before you were born. I leaped into a Fashion Design program at the Community College. I loved the fabrics and sewing. It was so exciting working with models and designers. I had finished the second semester and discovered I was pregnant. I dropped out, knowing I wouldn't be able to continue my dream once I was a mother."

"And here I thought it was something I had done. You were in class one day and gone the next. I was worried."

Gloria scrutinized her mom who was staring at Stan. They continued to gaze at each other until her mom lowered her eyes and walked from the kitchen into the living room. Gloria followed her and saw that Nick had done the same.

"I have a story to tell," her mom said and stopped next to the bookshelf. "You better sit Sweetie. And Stan, you need to hear this too."

Not sure what her mom wanted to say, Gloria plopped down on the couch and folded her arms across her chest. Nick stationed himself behind her and Belle continued laying on the floor. Stan hesitantly entered the room with his hands clasped behind his back, which was his normal posture when he was upset. She had seen it often in the last few years at work.

"Before I continue," her mom paused and moisten her lips. "I want you both to know I did what I believed was the best."

"Carol—"

"Stan no. It's time for me to stop living a lie," her mom said and dug out of a drawer in the bookshelf a brown legal sized envelope. "Gloria, the man you know as your father isn't, wasn't your father. It was why he left us on your eighteenth birthday."

"What!" Gloria sprung to her feet. This caused Belle to bark. Nick hushed Belle by crouching next to her and petting her. She glared at her mom. Her father wasn't her father? The man she had been angry at all these years for leaving them. What had the ghost Mr. Rouge said? Seeing some things from different angles could make things clearer. This was definitely from a view point she hadn't expected.

"I can't say how sorry I am. Every year it got harder to tell you." Her mom's voice cracked, and she saw her eyes watering.

"Mom, you are frightening me."

"I'm so sorry, sweetie. Your father—the man you know as your father had done a 23 and Me test on you and him. He wanted to surprise you with the information of your heritage as a birthday gift. I didn't know he had done it until the results came in the mail."

"Oh my God, I'm not liking were this is going, Mom," she hissed and ran a hand through her hair. Nick stood and placed a hand on her shoulder, and she covered it with hers.

"I had been—your dad—the man you've called dad and I had begun dating before I undertook my night school classes. A few months into our relationship, things changed. We fought all the time. He didn't want me going to school, saying it was a waste of time. When I refused to quit, he broke-up with me. Stan, who was in my classes had asked me out often," her mom paused and looked at him. "He was kind and always paid attention to what I had to say. I said yes. And things got hot and heavy quickly. We had—we had sex."

Gloria's eyes widened and she stiffened. "Ugg. I don't need to know who you had sex with once upon a time, mom. But you and my boss—Mr. Rouge?"

"Yes. We saw each other five days a week, plus whenever we went to the library to do research. I fell in love—I felt things I never did with Fred. Your dad—Fred and I reunited when Stan went to Paris for fashion week. I couldn't go. I didn't have enough money to study abroad."

"Two men? Mom really?"

"It wasn't that way. I was true to Fred when we were going out. And then to Stan. But when Stan came home from Paris and said he'd been offered an internship, I knew I couldn't hold him back. News of our baby would ruin him, so I walked out of his life and quit school."

Gloria frowned. "So, you dated when you were in school. That's interesting. Why is it so important to tell me now?"

"Because you need to know," her mom hesitated, looked at Stan then at Gloria. "Goodness, I don't know. Oh, I'm just saying it. It's past time I did. I'd like to introduce you to your real father."

"Wow! No way. No. No. I'm dreaming again. Mr. Rouge, take me back to my time." He looked at her like she had spoken in a different language. He stepped further into the living room.

"Ms. White—Gloria, this is the first time I'm hearing this as well. Carol, why didn't you tell me?"

"I—you were going places. Your designs were spectacular. I couldn't take that away from you. It is all my fault."

"Your fault? It takes two," Stan interjected. "I would have married you. None of my career means more to me then you. Even being the silent partner of the Crat-Chit clothing company. You have been the missing piece in my life, Carol."

"See. That's why I didn't tell you, Stan. Always the responsible one. I quit college when I found out I was pregnant. I resumed dating Fred. I lied to him. God forgive me. I told him he was the father. After that, the lie became the truth. His enthusiasm of becoming a father was off the charts. He never questioned if the child was his or not. It worked out because Gloria arrived past her true due date. The calculated time difference was marginalized in all the excitement of her birth, and it fit into Fred being the father."

Stan walked over to her mom and took her hands. "I would have been excited too. We could have worked through things, Carol."

"Wait a minute, you two. Mr. Rouge, sorry I can't call you dad or Stan, you own the Chat-Chit clothing company?"

"I do. The store you—we work at is my new design location. I wanted to expand some additional lines. That's why I came to the store."

"None of this makes any sense. The last twenty-four hours doesn't." Gloria took a step toward her mom. "What is in the envelope?"

"The results of the 23 and Me test. It shows you don't have any chromosomes that matched your father-Fred's."

"You've kept the results and your suspicions from me for all these years? For thirty-five years? You know how hard I took dads' leaving us. How it had affected me."

"I tried to tell you then, but you wouldn't listen to me. You went away to college. Then it just got more difficult to find the right moment. I'm so sorry."

Her mom began crying. She let her, but Mr. Rouge drew her close. Seeing the two of them in an embrace produced several degrees of hurt and betrayal. Her boss was her dad and owned a nationwide clothing company.

What was the universe trying to tell her?

Had fate intervened too?

"Mom, give me that envelope."

Stan released her mom, and she slowly lifted her arm. Grabbing the brown envelope, Gloria tore it open.

In big bold letters it said 100% not a match. The words

blurred together as tears clouded her eyes. She peered at Mr. Rouge and then her mom. "Why?"

The one-word question hung in the air. No one spoke. The only thing that broke the silence was Belle's panting.

"Maybe I should leave," Nick said.

"No, you are part of this, too. I was rude and mean to you the night my dad-Fred left us. You had asked for my number at Juicy Lucy's, but I never gave it to you. I was mad at the male species. Then there was the night you changed my tire. We kissed and I never called you."

Nick took a step closer to her. "You remember all that?"

"I didn't until last night when I hit my head. It all uncoiled from deep in my mind and re-emerged in full force. Like in fifth-grade, you were ready to put glue on Richard's chair for rejecting me in front of the class."

"For real? That was twenty-four years ago, Gloria. I wasn't sure you even knew who I was in grade school or middle school. I wanted you as my girlfriend so bad." Nick shook his head. "Man, that had been the turning point for me. I pieced together plans to make you like me."

"I ignored you, I know. I'm sorry. There were more times I was out-right rude to you, but you never gave up on me. I see that now. We've come full circle, you and I. You are the man I'm meant to be with forever."

"Are you proposing to me, Gloria?"

She laughed. Mr. Rouge, or whoever it had been that had been in her dreams, had been dead-on. Love had been right in front of her all this time, and she'd been too oblivious to see it until now.

"I guess, I am." She walked over to him, took his hands into hers. "Nick Klaaws, will you marry me?"

"You don't know how long I've waited to ask you. Now

you're asking me," he paused and met her gaze. "Yes. Yes, Gloria White, I would be honored to be your husband."

She smiled as he bent his head and captured her lips with his. Throwing her arms around him, she held him tight, afraid he might vanish, and that this was all a dream.

CHAPTER
FIFTEEN
SIX MONTHS LATER

Looking out of one of the tent panels, Gloria saw the sun was beginning its descent to the horizon. Its rays reached the sandy beach, causing the pebbles to sparkle. A gentle gulf breeze rustled the white gauze and sprays of flowers on the wedding trussell, setting a few feet from her. She inhaled to settle the apprehensiveness that had suddenly surged through her.

"Oh, honey, you look like a princess."

She turned to greet her mom and spotted tears glistening in her eyes. "Don't cry. You'll make me cry, too."

"Sorry," her mom sniffled and fanned her face with her hand. "It's almost time. I love you so much. Do you need anything?"

"A pinch. I can't believe this is happening." She shook her head a little. "It's only been six months since we got engaged. And here I am on my half birthday, in a wedding dress."

"One that your biological dad created. It's incredible. The beads along the neckline and cap sleeves add a little nostalgic look to the dress with the lace. I can't even imagine how much it cost to make. He wouldn't tell me." Her mom stepped over to her and tucked a wayward strand of hair into place, then took her hands. "You never were one to wait for things. All I know is that this seems right. Nick is a wonderful man. He's kind. Thoughtful. And gentle. He'll make a fantastic partner. And a great son-in-law to me."

"Why did it take me so long to realize all that? I wouldn't have gone through the hurt of breaking up with Jacob and all his baggage. I have been so stupid and so insensitive."

"No, no Sweetie. I'm partially to blame. I kept the truth of who your real father was from you. I didn't want you to think bad of me. Things were different back then. Being a single mom wouldn't have been an ideal situation. Love is strange. Look how long it took me to find Stan again."

"That's true. I don't know if I will get to the point of calling him dad, though," Gloria said and slipped on a pair a flat white sandals.

"He's not worried. He is just happy to be a part of yours and my life after all these years."

"I can't believe he is part owner of Chat-Chit Clothing stores. Ever since my promotion we've been working well together. He has been asking for my opinion on designs. It's been very exciting."

"It doesn't surprise me," her mom declared. "I knew he would become well known in the fashion world. Like I said his designs were so—so fabulous. I'm sure he had his pick of companies to work for back in the day. He was that good."

"Some of our time at the store working together is finally making sense. I thought Mr. Rouge—Stan was just being a mean boss, but he was doing things to protect the brand and to make the company better. I see that now. Do you think he would walk me down the aisle?"

Her mom gasped. "You will have to ask him."

"Will you ask him to come inside?"

"Of course."

Gloria pressed her hand flat to the front of the dress to smooth an invisible wrinkle. Having hemmed and hawed about asking him to be her escort, she knew it was the right thing to do. He was her father, even if they'd only known each other for two years. The reason they didn't have a relationship wasn't his fault. And he should be able to partake in the most important part of being a father in a wedding.

The panel opened and the man who had been tough on her at work and in her hellish nightmarish dreams, came into the tent. He didn't look like her boss dressed in a blue summer weight suit and white shirt opened at the neck, but a nervous father.

This was a new beginning. Time for new memories.

He stood tall and regal. No wonder her mom had fallen in love with him years ago. He hadn't lost his good looks, which was for sure. She should be proud to call him dad.

"Gloria, is something wrong with the dress?"

"No, Mr. Rouge—Staann. I'm sorry, the Mr. Rouge is a force of habit. I'm not ready to call you dad yet."

"That's okay. I understand. If and when you're ready to, is fine with me. What can I do for you? Carol—your mother didn't say why you needed me."

"Thank you for designing this dress. It is perfect." She took a step closer to him. "I was wondering if you…will you do me the honor of walking me down the aisle?"

His eyebrows lifted upward and then he smiled. "Wow. It would be my joy and honor. Are you sure?"

"Yes, we have a foundation, now we need to turn that into a relationship. But I want Sundays and Mondays off."

"Playing favorites isn't something I'm good at," Stan mumbled and then coughed to cover his emotions. "But I will make it work."

She laughed and wiped at a tear. "I think it's time we made our appearance."

"Goodness, then by all means let's give them a show." He extended his arm and she wrapped hers through his. "My heart is bursting with joy seeing you in the dress. There are no words to describe how absolutely—"

"Shhhh, you'll make me cry and ruin my makeup."

He patted her arm, and her mom chose that moment to open the tent's panel. A knowing look appeared on her face when she comprehended the meaning of their arms intertwined.

Stan led her out and they walked across a wide path of scattered rose petals on the sand. Their sweet fragrance reminded her of a day long ago that the ghost Mr. Rouge hadn't taken her to. Nick had given her a single rose on their last day of school in the eighth-grade. He had met her at her locker and handed it to her. His words boomeranged full circle to her.

I hope you think of me whenever you smell roses.

"Stan, do you believe in second chances?"

"I do. You are living proof."

"I want you to know I'm grateful for all your words of advice."

They reached the back row of chairs and the guests stood and turned to look at them.

"I'm not sure for what words, but it's your time now. Take

a deep breath. Keep your eyes on the man you love who is waiting for you."

Gloria did as he said. In and out, she breathed.

Raising her glance past the guests, she met Nick's eyes. He stood smiling with Belle next to him. She stared at him longingly and saw his gaze change. Gone was the happy look, it had become bold and seductive. Then it turned into a soft caress.

Her body tingled as his eyes shifted to her face, then downward to her shoulders, and to her exposed cleavage. Her pulse quickened.

This was the man she'd waited her entire life to love.

As they neared him, Belle barked, and the intensity of the moment was gone. They came to a stop within arm's reach of each other. The officiant took center stage.

"Welcome family and friends. We are here to celebrate two hearts that have found love. I'm told their journey has spanned decades. Beginning in the fifthgrade. Who says young love doesn't or won't last."

Laughter and some giggles erupted from the guests. Gloria couldn't help but smile. If she hadn't had her Christmas Carol nightmare, she would still be looking for love.

"Who is here to give this bride away to the groom?"

Stan tightened his fingers on her arm. "She doesn't need permission." He removed his hand and placed hers in Nick's outstretched hand. "Gloria is a very independent woman and only with her acknowledgement, do I, her dad, give her hand in marriage to Nick."

She turned to look at Mr. Rouge and thought for a moment she had seen the ghost version Mr. Rouge. Smiling at his heartfelt words, she blew him a kiss before facing the love of her life.

Nick folded his fingers around hers. "It has been my life-long dream that we get married, Gloria."

"It took me a while to get here, but it is I who is honored that you've waited for me."

"They stole the words from me," the officiate said.

Again, the guests laughed.

"In 1 Corinthians 13, it says love is patient. Love is also kind. What is love? It does not envy or boast. Nor is it proud. It's never rude. Love will always protect, trust, and give hope. Love never fails. Gloria and Nick are proof this is real," the officiate took their joined hands. "As you exchange rings, I ask you to pledge your love to each other."

"Gloria, accept this ring as a symbol of my love. And from this day forward be my wedded wife," he said and slid a gold band onto her finger.

"Nick, this ring is only a token of my love. May my love surround you during sickness and health. And until death do we part," she placed a matching band on his finger.

They looked at each other and said, "I do."

"Before God and those present, I have witnessed Nick's and Gloria's pledges to each other. By the authority given to me, I'd like to introduce you to Gloria and Nick Klaaws. And you may kiss as a symbol of your pledges."

Nick put his hands on her waist, and she glided her hands up higher on his chest. "I love you."

"I love you too."

His warm lips crushed over hers. Lost in the embrace, they didn't hear the shouts and whistles. Nothing mattered. She had found the man who had been destined to be her soulmate with the help of unseen forces.

Fate was indeed on her side.

Don't miss out on your next favorite book!

Join the Satin Romance mailing list
www.satinromance.com/mail.html

THANK YOU FOR READING

Did you enjoy this book?

We invite you to leave a review at your favorite book site, such as Goodreads, Amazon, Barnes & Noble, etc.

DID YOU KNOW THAT LEAVING A REVIEW…

- Helps other readers find books they may enjoy.
- Gives you a chance to let your voice be heard.
- Gives authors recognition for their hard work.
- Doesn't have to be long. A sentence or two about why you liked the book will do.

ABOUT THE AUTHOR

Born and raised in the cold and beautiful Minnesota, she escaped to Illinois for seventeen years to raise two boys, and now calls Florida home. She and her husband Andy, who's always her hero, have a new family to worry about; Cookie, an Assui-Po dog, Oreo, a black and white cat who thinks he is a dog, and Chip, a ragdoll cat, that their sons compare to Eeyore.

She loves to travel, read, and bowl. You can catch her writing her next novel at the lanes.

Sonja encourages you to check out her web site for more info and don't be surprised if she lets her Norwegian heritage come through in her stories. You betcha!

www.sonjagunter.com

ALSO BY SONJA GUNTER
WITH SATIN ROMANCE

Anthologies

First Class All the Way

in From Florida with Love, Sunsets & Happy Endings

Fast Lane Court Order

in From Florida with Love, Sunrise & Stormy Skies

Apple Pie Delight

in Food & Romance Go Together, Vol. 1